Carl Wrentham made the discovery of a life time. His new invention could change human civilization, bring enormous benefits to humanity as a whole, and make him a very rich man. But first he'd have to work out a few troublesome kinks.

MANAGANSETT PRESS

Don D'Ammassa is the author of:

Horror
Blood Beast
Servant of Chaos*
Caverns of Chaos*
Wings over Manhattan
The Gargoyle
That Way Madness Lies*
Little Evils*
Passing Death*
Date with the Dark*
The Devil Is in the Details*
Living Things*

Science Fiction
Scarab*
Haven*
Narcissus*
Translation Station
The Sinking Island*
Alien & Otherwise*
Wormdance*
Sandcastles*
Carbon Copies*

Mysteries
Murder in Silverplate*
Dead of Winter*
Death at the Art Gallery*
Death on the Mountain*
Death on Black Island*
Death in Black and White

Fantasy
The Kaleidoscope*
Elaborate Lies*
The Maltese Gargoyle*
Perilous Pursuits*
Multiplicity*

Nonfiction
The Encyclopedia of Science Fiction
The Encyclopedia of Fantasy and
Horror
The Encyclopedia of Adventure Fiction
Masters of Detection Vol I*
Masters of Detection Vol II*
Architects of Tomorrow Vol I*

*published by Managansett Press

CARBON COPIES

Don D'Ammassa

STAGES OF DEVELOPMENT

Carbon Copy	7
Copy Cat	22
Misprints	42
Transmission Errors	57
Backup Copies	83
Knockoffs	110
Proliferation	126
Double Exposure	148

CARBON COPIES

Part I: CARBON COPY

Evan Bruner's life might have developed in much the fashion he had long expected had he not allowed his wife to talk him into attending the costume party. He'd been working long hours at the hospital all month and tried to beg off but Kirsten had been looking forward to it and he knew she'd sulk for weeks if he spoiled her fun. It had happened in the past and would undoubtedly happen again, but this time he just wasn't up to facing the hurt looks, awkward silences, and occasional theatrical weepiness that would follow if he thwarted her.

Kirsten never missed an opportunity to dress up and show off, either personally or by proxy. She still had the collection of dolls she'd accumulated before they were married, with multiple outfits for each, even added to it occasionally. Evan's father had suggested a time or two that they were surrogates, since she was physically unable to have children, but Evan knew that wasn't the truth of the matter. Or at least not the whole truth. If they'd had kids Kirsten would probably have dressed them up instead, at least until they were too old to tolerate it, but it was the rearrangement of physical objects that motivated her. If anything, the children would have been surrogates for the dolls. Kirsten's domineering father had ordered every aspect of her life until cancer ended his reign of order and control. It was permanently imprinted on his daughter and Evan sometimes wonder if she had accepted his proposal simply because she could not summon the will to deny him. It was an unspoken uncertainty that made him feel guilty whenever he had to deny her something she wanted.

So Evan reluctantly agreed to go to the party at the Boncoddos. Kirsten fitted him for his costume over the course of a week, white silk blouse and black pantaloons, a thick red cummerbund to disguise the incipient paunch, a patch across one eye, a plastic cutlass at his waist. She'd also bought a toy parrot that she wanted to pin to his shoulder, but he'd balked and Kirsten had pouted but accepted defeat.

Evan was expecting his wife to dress as a fairy princess or the Queen of England, but she surprised him, having kept her personal plans secret so that she could reveal them at the last possible moment. He was downstairs practicing walking without catching the faux sword between his legs when he heard the bedroom door open upstairs and footsteps cross the landing. He looked up, blinked, and for a moment thought Kirsten must have invited another costumed guest to stop by on her way to the party.

They had been married almost ten years, and Evan had seen his wife in scores, perhaps hundreds of different sets of clothing. She'd worn dresses and skirts, shorts and slacks, bathing suits and business suits, formal gowns that clung and informal sweats that hung. He had almost never known her to appear unattractive, but there had never been more than a hint of the lascivious. Kirsten wasn't prudish by nature, but she was modest in public. She didn't own a bikini, let alone a thong. Her skirts were often unstylishly long and she hadn't been willing to sunbathe in the backyard until Evan finished building the trellises that ensured none of the neighbors could enjoy the view. In many ways, Evan thought of her as still a child bride, and in his more introspective moments he realized that he had married a sweet, affectionate, but not particularly bright woman who had never and would never completely grow up.

So it came as quite a surprise to see her dressed as a harem girl.

Her face was covered, of course, by a filmy, rose colored swatch of cloth that wrapped around behind her head. So were her hips, just barely. And her breasts, even less barely. Or maybe more barely. He could probably have rolled her entire costume up into a ball and stuffed it into a pocket. A shirt pocket. Kirsten was only five feet tall, barely one hundred pounds. It didn't take much to cover her up. Even less to partially cover her up.

Ornate pins held the material in place, one in the center of her chest, the other poised like a chastity belt. She was wearing sandals, ruby red, with straps that wrapped around her legs in overlapping strands that came up to just above her knees. Her hair was done in a style he'd never seen before, almost all of it held to the left side of her head, fixed there with yet another jeweled pin. There was a loose silver bracelet on her left wrist and a matching one on her right ankle. Evan suddenly had another reason for not wanting to spend the evening with John and Emily Boncoddo and their friends. He even made some suggestions to that effect, all of which were quietly ignored.

Evan was experiencing troublesome misgivings before they left the house. He was rather pleased by the idea that his male neighbors would envy him such a beautiful wife. On the other hand, he wasn't entirely sure that he was going to enjoy noticing other men looking at her in her present attire. But he'd agreed to go and other than a broad hint that she might be a little overexposed, he made no protest.

They got past the initial greetings without incident. John shook Evan's hand and drew him inside, making some crack about forgetting to explain that guests were supposed to bring their own wives rather than mysterious, seductive women. Evan decided not to respond with anything more than a slight smile. About a dozen people were scattered through the house, and voices suggested a few more out by the pool. He recognized most of them but couldn't always recall their names. Emily was a skilled hostess, though. "Evan, you remember Bill and Kathy Warren, don't you? And Dave Driscoll is here somewhere as well."

He shook hands, accepted a drink, nodded to a vampire and a witch, and looked for a quiet corner. Kirsten liked to hold court at parties and once Evan found a suitable place for her to sit, she was unlikely to move again before it was time to go home. All of the seats inside were taken at first, but there was a slow migration toward poolside as the heat of the day finally began to relent, and when the love seat in one corner emptied, he turned to usher his wife to her throne.

But she wasn't where she was supposed to be. She had quietly slipped away from his side and stood near the sliding door to the pool area, talking to someone whose face was hidden by a thick, patently false beard, and a jeweled turban. Evan dodged Judge Carpenter, who was already red faced and unsteady on his feet, and joined them. Even from close at hand, it took a second or two before he recognized Carl Wrentham, who had moved into the last house on Maple Street six months earlier. They had spoken briefly once or twice, but all he knew about the man was that he was some kind of independent researcher.

"Evening, Carl. How are the renovations coming?" He'd bought the Linville house despite its poor condition and there had been a regular procession of contractors ever since.

Wrentham shrugged noncommittally. "The worst of it has been taken care of, and I've been too busy to worry about the rest. I was just telling your wife here that we make a good pair." His hand rose to tap his turban. "Costumewise only, of course."

Carl laughed at his own joke. Evan didn't even bother with a smile. "So what have you been up to?"

"This and that." It had been clear from their first meeting that Evan didn't want to discuss his work. "Say, we're blocking traffic here. Why don't we go outside?" He took Kirsten's arm and adroitly maneuvered her through the door. Evan was left to fend for himself and followed in their wake, disproportionately irritated.

"Would you get me a glass of wine, Evan?" Kirsten's perfectly reasonable request made things even worse. Evan poured a glass of Merlot for Kirsten, knowing she didn't care for it, and a brandy for himself.

It took a few seconds to track them down. Carl and Kirsten had worked their way to the far side of the pool and were now stretched out on lawn chairs in the shadow of the utility shed. Evan handed Kirsten her wine and stood deliberately between them. There was no chair for him. The evening was going rapidly from bad to horrible. Kirsten and Carl got along entirely too well – he had never seen her so animated -- and Evan finally began circulating because he couldn't stand to watch it any longer. He wasn't afraid that Kirsten would cheat, but she'd never even flirted before, and that was obviously what she was doing with Carl Wrentham. It was as though the change in costuming had changed her personality as well.

She drank more than usual. So did Evan, who offended one of the neighbors with a too candid comment about some political issue she was expounding upon. He regretted it immediately but didn't trust himself to attempt to smooth things over. It was more likely that he'd make things even worse.

He was about to pour another drink when he spotted Carl Wrentham heading for the front door, obviously on his way out. He was quite pleased until he noticed that Kirsten was accompanying him. He moved to intercept them.

"What's up guys?" he asked with exaggerated casualness.

Kirsten looked neither startled nor guilty. "Carl's going to show me something he built. Wanna come with us?"

"It's not that big a deal," mumbled Carl, who most assuredly did look guilty, and mildly belligerent. Evan sensed that Carl was not used to drinking. His face was flushed and he was clearly unsteady on his feet.

"I was thinking maybe it's time for us to go home. I've got an early surgery tomorrow."

"Oh, this won't take long, will it, Carl?" Kirsten waved her arm vaguely.

Evan tried to dissuade her, but even Carl's obvious second thoughts failed to inhibit her enthusiasm. There was nothing Evan could do but follow his unusually animated wife and his disgruntled neighbor down the street, through the gate, and up onto the porch of an oversized Victorian mess of a house. Carl didn't need to use his key to get in. "I always forget to lock up," he explained. "Or I lock the door and forget to take the key with me."

The house was dark but not so dark that Evan couldn't tell there was almost no furniture. They followed their host through the kitchen to a doorway that was almost hidden behind a row of shelves, then down a narrow staircase. Evan was expecting the dimly lit, damp, and dirty basement where Tom Linville had kept his tools and his fishing gear, but it had been completely transformed. There was a new, almost spotless concrete floor, the walls were paneled, the ceiling covered by acoustic tiles, and at the far end was what looked like a modern electronics workshop and a row of large, unidentifiable pieces of equipment, some of them resembling gigantic fish tanks.

"Like Marie Curie, I discovered one thing while looking for something else entirely," Carl said quietly, but with a hint of enthusiasm finally animating his voice. "We were trying to develop a viable desalinization process, you know, taking the salt out of salt water, and I noticed an odd anomaly. The lab where I worked at the time didn't want to pursue what they considered a side issue of no consequence, so I bought some equipment and experimented on my own. Here, I'll show you."

Carl almost tripped over his own feet, recovered himself, opened the door to one of the two largest glass walled chambers. They were each about the size of a telephone booth. He looked around, then took a circuit board from a nearby shelf. He placed it on the floor inside the chamber and closed the door. "This unit does the scan." The control toggle was large and green but unlabelled. A moment after Carl touched it, there was a faint hum but no other perceptible change. The sound stopped almost immediately. "Now that it's recorded, we can generate the copy, if we have enough raw materials." He turned to a computer terminal mounted between the two chambers. The screen was full of indecipherable data, but a green light blinked in the upper left hand corner. "Green means we have adequate raw materials in storage, so…" He pressed another toggle, this one blue.

A light blinked on, illuminating a second chamber that was virtually identical to the first. The hum returned for a couple of seconds, with a slightly different pitch, then died. Carl opened the door to chamber two, crouched and reached in, then held up his hand to display what he'd found there. A circuit board.. "The original is still in the other chamber." He opened that door and then held up the two identical objects so that they could see them. His grin of triumph was just slightly asymmetrical, and his red face detracted from the overall effect.

Evan used to read science fiction, so he responded almost immediately. "Matter duplication?" He figured it was an elaborate parlor trick and his skepticism must have been apparent because Carl's back stiffened.

"Not exactly. Oh, I could make an exact duplicate of a gold bar if I had one, all right, but to do that, I'd have to have an equal quantity of gold in elemental storage first. It's reassembly, not transmutation. I can't get rich that way. And yes, I could duplicate paper money, but how long do you think it would take before someone noticed an anomalous number of bills with identical serial numbers?"

"How about diamonds?" Evan challenged. "They're just carbon."

Carl's eyes drifted away and he seemed to shrink down a size or two. "I can make diamonds, sure. But I haven't perfected the process yet. There are small errors." His speech was rapidly becoming more slurred. "The diamonds would have flaws. Electronics don't work right either, chips or transistors. This one is junk." He waved the second circuit board at them. "I have to develop more accurate readings. Then I'll be able to make anything I want."

"You don't really expect us to believe this, do you?" Evan was growing angry. He'd had too much to drink and he was sure that Carl had been planning to make a move on his wife. Even more upsetting, Kirsten seemed to be responding on some level. Evan wanted to break Carl's nose, but even the prospect of physical violence always upset him.

"How about animals?" asked Kirsten, apparently oblivious to the effluvia of dueling testosterone.

Carl's face grew more animated. "Sure. I tried it on a stray cat. I still have the scanned data." He typed something on the keyboard, backing up twice to correct errors. When the green light appeared, he turned and slapped the blue toggle, and chamber two hummed again. When it stopped, a good sized cat lay inside. Carl opened the door and carefully lifted it out. Evan could tell that it was breathing, but it was completely limp.

"I call it my Copy Cat. It's not really alive, not exactly," said Carl, even as he stroked its coat. "The duplicate is organically correct as far as I can tell, but everything living that I've tried – mice, insects – they all end up like this. The body seems to have some kind of residual momentum – it has a pulse and it breathes, but after ten hours or so, it just stops." He walked slowly to a large, blocky metal structure that vaguely resembled an old fashioned furnace. With his free hand he pulled down a hopper mounted on one side, and with the other he tossed the cat – if that's what it was – inside. "All of the raw materials get recycled," he explained. "Broken down to the base elements and stored for reuse."

Evan turned to Kirsten, expecting to see her reeling with horror, but to his surprise she was leaning forward, eyes wide, obviously fascinated. "What would happen if you did it to a person?"

At first Evan found the idea completely repulsive, but then he began to wonder as well. He felt compelled to say something about the ethical implications, but Carl seemed lost in thought, as though he had never really considered such a thing, or had managed to push the possibility to the back of his mind where he could pretend it didn't exist. Then Kirsten precipitated a crisis by turning and climbing into chamber one.

"Come out of there, Kirsten. It's time to go home." Evan was angry, the angriest he had ever been with her, but if she noticed, she paid no attention.

"Copy me, Carl. I want to see what I look like without using a mirror."

Evan wasn't expecting Carl to cooperate, and desperately wanted to take his wife out of this place. Even without the benefit of Carl's electronic wizardry she was changing into something else right in front of his eyes. He crossed to the chamber, swung the door open, reached inside and took hold of her right wrist. There was a humming noise.

There was no physical sensation; the scanning process was imperceptible. The sound immobilized him for a moment, and then he pulled his protesting wife out of the chamber so roughly that she glared at him. Her face was flushed and she might have shouted at him, but then there was a second hum from the other chamber, as Carl completed the process, apparently anxious to see the results now that he had committed himself. "We were lucky," he said afterward. "I was afraid we might be missing some of the trace elements. I fill the hopper regularly with all kinds of organic matter, grass clippings, garbage, even road kill, but you never know what might come up short."

A second Kirsten Crowley had materialized in chamber two, immediately falling over onto one side. Her chest was rising and falling regularly but the eyes were closed and remained that way. Evan watched it for several seconds, then turned away and vomited onto Carl's nice clean floor. When he turned back, wiping his mouth with the back of his sleeve, Kirsten was standing over her twin. Clutching the duplicate's right arm was a hand, Evan's hand, ending at the wrist. The stump looked as though it had been cauterized.

"She's beautiful," said Kirsten.

An indeterminate period of frozen time went by. "What are you going to do with it?" Evan asked hoarsely.

Carl looked sick, as though he hadn't thought out the consequences of what he'd just done. "I'll have to put it in the hopper. Reclaim the raw materials." His voice was brittle, raw.

"It won't fit," Evan pointed out, suppressing a bizarre urge to giggle.

Carl squared his shoulders and drew a deep breath. "Then I'll just have to cut it up first."

Neither Evan nor Kirsten brought up the subject the next day. They barely even mentioned the party and certainly didn't allow Carl Wrentham's name to pass their lips. But something had changed in their relationship. It was obvious to both of them. Evan told himself that it was a transient thing, to be forgotten completely within days, but he felt a totally unfamiliar and unwelcome sense of loss.

Weeks passed during which he failed to convince himself that they were getting back to normal. Kirsten began to act strangely. Sometimes she'd be withdrawn, moody, even depressed; on other occasions she was animated, upbeat, almost frantic. He started calling home during the day and there were numerous occasions when no one answered the telephone. Kirsten insisted that she'd been napping, or working in the yard, or had walked down to the grocery store – she had never learned to drive. She daydreamed constantly and while she never said or did anything he could point to specifically, it was clear that she had changed in some significant fashion. The weeks turned to months and Evan slowly came to the conclusion that she was having an affair, and the prime candidate was Carl Wrentham. So he decided to catch them in the act.

The hospital was experimenting with work cycles and Evan was senior enough to do some creative scheduling. He arranged things to allow for irregular half days off. On each of these occasions, he drove to the shopping center half a mile from the house, parked, and walked the back way so that he could reach his own neighborhood unobserved. There were plenty of places to hide and watch.

On his fourth attempt, Evan saw Kirsten leave the house, carrying a garment bag over one shoulder. She turned at the end of the driveway and started toward Carl's house. He watched from concealment as she climbed onto Carl's porch and went inside, without knocking, then followed, approaching carefully so that he couldn't be seen if someone looked out the front window.

The curtains were drawn on all the downstairs windows except the kitchen, and those that looked down into the basement had been painted over. The back porch was small and narrow and in poor repair; two of the boards creaked underfoot despite his exaggerated care. But the back door was unlocked, both screen and interior, and with his heart throbbing wildly Evan slipped into the house.

There were voices coming from the basement, which spared him the chore of searching. He paused at the top of the steps but could only make out scattered words, occasional light laughter, and the deeper tones of Carl's voice. So he started to inch down the stairs until he could see what they were doing.

Carl had made another copy of Kirsten, presumably from the template he'd created on that first occasion. The copy stood on a small platform, erect only because her – its arms were draped over a wooden framework. The disembodied hand had already been removed. The copy wasn't wearing the harem outfit, however. She was dressed in an off--the--shoulder gown. Kirsten, the real Kirsten, was doing something to her hair. She had turned the duplicate of her own body into a life sized, living doll.

Evan almost gave himself away when he bolted from the scene, but they must have been too preoccupied to notice whatever sounds he made. He vomited in the bushes in Carl's backyard, without benefit of booze this time, and when Kirsten finally came home, he was lying in bed. "Came home sick," he explained, and she never questioned it.

Over the course of the next few weeks, Evan followed Kirsten to Carl's house six more times. The back door was never locked and each visit was a variation of the first. Sometimes the duplicate was posed lying down, or seated, sometimes dressed for winter, sometimes for summer. Kirsten even bought a bikini. She never wore it, but her duplicate did. On three occasions, there were two dolls for her to play with. The second was a duplicate of Carl Wrentham. Carl didn't appear to participate except as a spectator.

It must have been a different duplicate every time, of course. Carl had said that organic copies only lasted a few hours. But she always looked exactly the same. Evan never saw any evidence that Kirsten was actually being unfaithful to him, but what he did see seemed somehow even worse, more perverted than simply screwing a neighbor. On some level, this was an even greater betrayal.

Kirsten began taking fewer pains with her own appearance. Evan watched her go outside to retrieve the newspaper one morning with curlers in her hair. Such informality was completely unlike her. Her marvelous clothing sense had given way to mismatches and color clashes. It was as though she were expending all of her stylish instincts on the duplicates, with nothing left for herself. She hadn't touched her dolls in weeks.

Evan knew he had to do something, but as with most things in his life, he was careful, deliberate, and painstaking. He stole a lethal dose of a drug from the hospital by extracting tiny amounts from separate ampoules, slowly accumulating enough for one application and then, just to be on the safe side, added enough for a second, just in case the first syringe malfunctioned. Any competent medical examiner would spot the drug, of course, but he didn't intend that an autopsy would ever be performed on the body of Carl Wrentham.

The hospital was hosting a conference of neurosurgeons and that suggested an alibi, not that Evan expected to need one. He left the clinic early that evening, promising to attend the reception at the Hilton as soon as he ran an errand.

It was near dark by the time he arrived at the shopping center. He carried a canvas bag to Carl's house, entered through the back door with the two syringes in his jacket pocket. The door to the basement was open, but the lights were off. Evan cursed silently. Carl couldn't have picked a worse time to go out. But he wasn't out. Evan had half turned away when he heard a sound from upstairs.

Old as the house was, it was solidly built. There was only one very faint creak as Evan mounted the stairs and made his way down the hall. He peered through the open door into the master bedroom. It was dark, but the moon was bright enough falling through the window to illuminate a roughly human shape lying in bed. Evan took a step through the doorway, froze when there was sudden movement. An arm rose and fell to one side and a dark haired head turned. He recognized Carl Wrentham's face and a moment of blind rage vanquished the last trace of hesitation.

Evan lunged across the room and plunged the point of a syringe through the sheet and into warm flesh. The drug worked quickly. Paralysis would be almost immediate. The heart and lungs would stop and Carl would be dead. Evan took a step back and waited, counting under his breath.

And Carl sat up.

For a moment, it was Evan's heart that almost stopped, but then the falling sheet revealed that there were two bodies in the bed. He felt confused and disoriented, but beneath the panic lay a kernel of cold reasoning. He brought out the second syringe and before Carl could say a word, Evan jabbed him in the thigh. Carl did say one word then, actually a single syllable. "Oh?" And then he fell back, dead almost before he hit the pillow.

Evan pulled off the sheet and had another bad moment. The second corpse was Kirsten! But then he recognized what she was wearing – or at least half wearing -- the harem outfit, and a wave of relief mixed with complete revulsion swept over him. Kirsten must have frustrated Carl by being so close but so unobtainable. He had, therefore, produced a copy to keep his bed warm, and perhaps for other purposes. Was this necrophilia, Evan wondered, or some entirely new perversion?

It took longer than he had expected since there were two bodies to dispose of instead of one, but Carl had a bathtub in the basement with an impressive array of tools useful in dismemberment. After disassembling the two bodies in the bathtub, Evan dropped each piece into the hopper to be recycled. Environmentally friendly body disposal. Then he threw in all the bed clothing, the pillows, and the two syringes. The canvas bag went last.

Evan was a methodical man. His profession had taught him to leave nothing to chance. Once the series of necessary but unpleasant chores was complete, he went to Carl's computer, searched until he discovered how to retrieve the profile he wanted, and then made a copy of the late Mr. Wrentham. He was relieved to see that the end product was appropriately dressed for an excursion. Wrestling the unresponsive body upstairs was more difficult than Evan had expected, however, and by the time he had the Carl duplicate on the front porch, he was drenched with sweat. Steeling himself to the task, he arranged the last chapter of his drama, made a quick mental review of everything that had been done, then went back to the shopping center, got into his car, and drove to the hotel.

He found it difficult to get into the spirit of the evening, but he managed.

An hour later he made an anonymous call to the police from a pay phone several blocks away. He claimed to have been driving down Maple Street and noticed that a man was lying unconscious in front of one of the houses. It looked like he might have fallen off the porch. They would find the pseudo--Carl still alive, of course, but unresponsive, and he would die from unknown causes in a few hours. There would be an autopsy to discover the cause of death, and heaven knows what they would find, but it wouldn't be a toxic drug or any other substance that might suggest murder.

And they would certainly never suspect that the body wasn't the real Carl Wrentham, because it was. Sort of.

Evan resisted the urge to celebrate by drinking too much at the reception. He forced himself to be congenial and patient even though he wanted to go home, to be there when Kirsten discovered that Carl was dead, that her larger than life fantasy world had come to an end. Evan wanted her full attention again, and told himself everything would be the way it was before.

Late that night, he came home to a dark, empty house on a dark, quiet street. The police and the ambulance had come and gone. He was puzzled by her absence at first, wondered if she had decided to go along with Carl's unresponsive body to the hospital. The possibility that she had left him for some reason persisted despite his attempts to dismiss it, so he went through her closets, was relieved to find her suitcases all safely stowed. As far as he could tell, all of her clothing was in place. Except for one outfit.

The harem costume. Realization hit him with such force that his knees wobbled and he sat down on the floor, shaking uncontrollably.

Evan thought about killing himself. He wasn't worried about being caught; he'd been too careful. But he wasn't sure that he wanted to face life alone knowing what he had done. Objectively he knew that Kirsten had never needed him the way he needed her, but that didn't make his grief any easier to deal with. The prospect of a life without her seemed too plain, ordinary, and uninteresting to contemplate.

Then he felt angry. He couldn't decide which hurt more, that Kirsten had at last betrayed him with Carl, or that he'd unwittingly killed her and would never see her again. The police came the next day to ask about Carl and he managed to compose himself. That seemed an appropriate time to announce that his wife was missing, that he had found her side of the bed empty that morning and was understandably upset. The apparent coincidence made them suspicious, of course, but somehow he managed to deal with them without giving anything away. It was as though an inner zombie had taken over his body. Eventually they left him alone.

A week went past. Then another. Every few days Detective Gates would stop by and ask some more questions or the same questions again. They searched the house and went over the yard very thoroughly. Carl's yard as well. Carl had died without leaving a will. It might take years to settle his estate.

Evan was so distracted that the hospital administration suggested a prolonged leave of absence. He agreed, went home, sat in his empty house, and cultivated his grief. And then one day it occurred to him that he could have Kirsten back again, at least for a while. All he had to do was break into Carl Wrentham's basement.

The police had secured the property but the back door was no match for a crowbar. Evan didn't dare show a light upstairs, but there were no windows in the basement, so he turned the switch as he descended the stairs. It was a relief when the power came on; if it had been otherwise, the duplicator would not have worked.

He booted the computer and waited impatiently until the menu appeared. It was easier to navigate the menus this time. He highlighted the profile titled "KIRST" and waited for the green light. There were adequate raw materials. Without hesitation, Evan pressed the blue toggle and a moment later he was rewarded with the familiar hum of the duplicator. Chamber two flashed and she was there and he pulled her out and hugged her. She was warm and soft and pliant and for the first few seconds it felt real. But she wouldn't respond or stand by herself and her dead weight pulled at him when he lifted her from the chamber and that dispelled the illusion. He lowered her body to the floor, sat down beside it, and cried for a while.

He wondered what would happen if he tried again. Carl had told them that the process was flawed, that the copies all had tiny variations. He had no expectation of getting back the wife he had known, but maybe he could find something a little closer, a little more aware. Evan walked over to the console and highlighted the profile again. The light went from green to red.

He turned and stared at the body lying on the floor, so much like and unlike Kirsten. Then he carried her over to the tub and began preparing her for the hopper.

There was no discernible difference between the first and second copies, or the third, or the fourth. Evan settled into the cycle of materialization, hope, disappointment, resolution, dismemberment, and back to the start. His clothing was sticky with blood, but he didn't care, and he lost count of how many times he had failed. It never occurred to him that the flaw was in the scanning, not the materialization, and that he could not succeed no matter how many times he tried.

Then the green light refused to come on any longer and he realized that it was an imperfect system. Blood and tissue covered him from head to foot, there were sticky puddles on the floor, more residue splashed on the walls. He had dropped below the point where he was recycling enough to create the next copy. There were things upstairs that he could throw into the hopper to make up the difference, but when he started to climb the steps, exhaustion hit so hard that he collapsed slowly to his knees, leaning forward with his head against the rough wood, and he couldn't find the strength to continue.

That's where the police found him a few hours later, lying in a charnel house. Evan realized instantly that they were going to conclude that he'd hidden his wife's body somewhere, and had been belatedly disposing of it. The thought struck him as funny and he began making a strange sound that might have been an expression of humor.

But if so, it was a poor copy of a laugh.

Part II: COPY CATS

Chloe Wrentham was between jobs when she inherited her uncle's house. She wasn't entirely surprised because Uncle Carl had favored her for as long as she could remember. He'd never married but he'd been close to his brother and her family and had treated Chloe as if she was his own daughter. They had drifted apart when she'd gone off to Michigan State University, but occasional letters and telephone calls had kept the link firmly in place, if attenuated.

She had majored in chemistry because that was her uncle's field, even though she had no real aptitude for it. When her parents died in a plane crash during her junior year, the loss of their financial support was the excuse rather than the reason that she dropped out. Their insurance would have paid for her expenses through graduation and Uncle Carl had offered to help out. She had insisted that she needed time off to come to terms with the loss of her parents, but actually she felt closer to her uncle than to either of them. She felt more grief over his death than theirs.

Carl Wrentham had accumulated a sizeable investment portfolio and Chloe realized that if she lived frugally, she wouldn't have to work. Although she still intended to pursue a career of some sort when she figured out what it was that she actually wanted to do with her life, there was no hurry. She came to Managansett to sell the house and decided that it was just as good a place to live as any while she was sorting herself out.

The basement smelled bad and after one quick look around, she closed the door leading downstairs with a vague idea of contacting someone to see if she could sell the laboratory equipment. The house was large – fifteen rooms – and her uncle's taste in furniture ran to straight lines and utility, so she spent the next couple of months rearranging and replacing until things suited her. She completely forgot about the basement and what it contained.

Until the day she started reading her uncle's journals.

Dennis Scoggins and his wife Victoria had lived on Myrtle Lane for ten years when their neighbor, Carl Wrentham, had died mysteriously. Myrtle was originally supposed to go right through the woods behind the Sheffield Library and connect up to Reservoir

Road, but the developer who started the project in 1969 was arrested for income tax evasion and by the time everything got sorted out, housing was in a slump and Managansett sure wasn't going to buck the trend. The town had no significant industry of its own except for Eblis Manufacturing, and it was just a bit too far from Providence for a convenient commute. So only five houses got built on Myrtle, which starts just past the rather seedy Victorian where Wrentham lived and ends rather abruptly facing a row of defiant pine trees.

The Blackwoods and the Touraines bought their houses new back in the 1970s and raised two kids each. Billy Blackwood – make that William Blackwood – married Jennifer Touraine and they were in Vermont raising two kids of their own. All four parents were retired now, although Jeanne Blackwood still did some consulting. Dennis and Victoria bought the house facing the Blackwoods when Edna Guilford died. Next to them was Abner Crane, a widower and something of a recluse, although he was always polite enough on those rare occasions when he was out and about.

A good ways past him was the Elliot place. Tabitha Elliot had vowed to die in that house, but Alzheimer's has a way of changing people's plans. The neighbors looked out for her as best they could and pretended that she was just getting forgetful, but then she started ringing doorbells at all hours of the night, asking if anyone had seen her husband Fred who had died back in 1981. So one day Dennis copied the daughter's phone number off the side of her refrigerator and made an awkward, painful call, and a few weeks later there was a For Sale sign out front that no one would ever see except for the neighbors, because the pavement stopped a few yards beyond and no one would ever drive by.

No one expected it to sell any time soon, but it was only three weeks before the sign came down, and as far as anyone could tell, no one had even come to look at the place. Victoria went down to the town hall and found out it had been bought by someone named Laurie Kaitan and sure enough, a week later a moving van drove past just as Dennis was sweltering in the humidity and wondering if a shower might help. Curious, he walked down to introduce himself but there was just a realtor and the moving people. The furniture was all tagged so they could leave things in the right room, but there was no sign of the owners.

Dennis was also the first to know when the new neighbor actually moved in. There had been a conference in Buffalo and he'd planned to spend the night and come back after the morning session on Saturday, but the program item he'd hoped to attend had been cancelled, so Dennis checked out, preferring to drive home and sleep in his own bed even if it meant arriving in the small hours of the morning. He was pretty worn out by the time he got home, but not so sleepy that he didn't notice the glow of light from the far end of Myrtle. Curious, he left his suitcase on the front porch and walked up the street to get a better look.

There were lights on at the Elliot house. It was actually the Kaitan house now, but like most Rhode Islanders, Dennis tended to identify landmarks by what they used to be rather than what they were at present. The front room and the kitchen downstairs were both lit up, and one room on the top floor. A Volkswagen van, not a new one, was parked in the driveway. It had Connecticut license plates and no bumper stickers. Ordinarily that would have been enough to satisfy his immediate curiosity, but just as he was about to turn around, he heard a peculiar noise that caught his attention. It stopped right away, but then repeated itself. It was the sound of nails ripping out of wood and it was coming from the garage. Someone was opening crates. Instinctively Dennis glanced at his watch, confirmed that it was almost three in the morning. Dennis shrugged. None of his business, after all. And then he turned and went home.

Dennis wasn't the first to actually meet the new neighbor. Michelle Touraine had acted with her usual decisiveness and appointed herself Welcoming Committee. It was Michelle's voice from the kitchen downstairs that woke him up. Michelle was a sweet woman but she'd been losing her hearing progressively for years, and her already deep, raspy voice was rising in volume in compensation. She was drinking tea with Victoria when Dennis came down, dressed but with his hair still wet from the shower. He nodded good morning and made a beeline for the coffee pot, which was rarely turned off despite his doctor's terse suggestion that he switch to decaf.

"Michelle just met our new neighbor," said Victoria.

Dennis sipped the coffee, strong and black, just the thing to convince his body that six hours of sleep was more than enough. "What's he like?"

"Well for one thing," Michelle almost shouted, "he's a she."

"Husband? Kids?" Dennis walked to the kitchen window facing the dead end, but it was more gravitational attraction than common sense. Abner Crane's house, two rows of poplars, and various other impediments blocked his view.

"It's just her. The husband died a while back; she didn't say how. Apparently she's a friend of Chloe Wrentham. And before you ask, she's in her twenties, average looks, polite but standoffish."

"She didn't offer Michelle tea," explained his wife.

"Ah! A critical mistake. Let's run her out of town." Dennis drifted over to the table and sat down. "She was probably exhausted. The house was all lit up when I got home late last night. I don't suppose she mentioned what she does for a living?"

"No," said Michelle, pouting a bit. Normally she would have elicited a new acquaintance's life story, including intimate moments, within minutes of meeting them. Laurie Kaitan must be formidable indeed. "But I noticed her books. Lots of stuff on electronics, the technical side, not consumer stuff."

"Maybe she's a mad scientist," Dennis suggested with a reasonably straight face.

"I wouldn't put it past her."

The trash collectors weren't happy when they reached Myrtle Lane for the next few weeks. Cardboard cartons, packing materials, and broken wooden crates were waiting for them every Thursday morning. They wouldn't take the wood, which they decided to consider construction materials, but Dennis took away some of it himself. The boards were in good shape and he was rebuilding the roof of the storage shed in his back yard. There were various names stenciled on some of them, but paint would cover that up.

Dennis was cutting the grass that afternoon and he noticed an unfamiliar pickup truck driving past the house. Curious, he stood and watched it as it pulled into the driveway at the Kaitan house. Two men got out and rang the doorbell. After a few seconds they went inside..

Dennis returned to his work and was about halfway done when he heard an engine start and looked up. The two men had placed a bulky object in the back of the truck, but Dennis couldn't see what it was because it was wrapped in a canvas tarp. They backed out and drove slowly past until they reached the intersection, then turned right. There were no trees at the corner and Dennis could see that they had pulled into the circular driveway in front of Chloe Wrentham's house. He glanced that way from time to time while he was finishing up and saw them unload their cargo and carry it toward the house.

He had just finished and was cleaning off the mower when Laurie Kaitan came out of her house, got into her Volkswagen, backed out into the street and turned, naturally, in his direction. Dennis was still trying to decide whether or not it would be appropriate to wave a greeting as she passed when the Volkswagen stopped in front of him. The driver rolled down her window and hailed him.

"Excuse me! Could you give me some directions?"

Dennis stood up straight, ignoring a twinge or two in his back, and walked over to the sidewalk. "I'll try. Where do you want to go?" Michelle's description hadn't been far off, but Dennis suspected that with a little makeup, a good night's rest, and a visit to a hairdresser, Laurie's appearance might rate something higher than average. "I'm Dennis Scoggins, by the way." He extended his hand.

She hesitated, but only for an instant. Her hand was cool and fragile, almost childlike. Dennis couldn't imagine them tearing open wooden crates. "Laurie Kaitan. I need a hardware store."

"Go back out to Main Street and turn right. Manny's Hardware doesn't look like much, but he's got a pretty good selection. Otherwise, go the other way along Route 13. There's a Benny's in the plaza at the town line."

She thanked him with the barest suggestion of a smile, then drove off. It all seemed very innocuous for his first encounter with a monster.

Not much changed on Myrtle Lane for the next few weeks. Laurie Kaitan spent much of her time visiting Chloe Wrentham and most of the rest working as an adjunct instructor at Brown University. There was a flurry of traffic– UPS, Federal Express, G.O.D. -- all delivering small and occasionally not so small packages. Most of these were delivered to Chloe Wrentham but a good number ended up sitting on Laurie Kaitan's front porch. The neighbors, if they thought about it all, assumed they were ordering things to furnish their houses. Despite four months residency, none of the neighbors had been inside Kaitan's house since Michelle's welcome visit.

The first odd thing happened almost two months later, and at the time it didn't seem very important. The Blackwoods had two cats, Yin and Yan. Yin was the extrovert; he came over to the neighbors occasionally to be petted. Yan kept to himself and he had a temper when roused. Both Ed and Jeanne had been scratched more than once, and Yan had taken a swipe at Dennis once when he had almost stepped on a whisking tail. They weren't housecats except during bad weather. Jeanne thought it was wrong to keep them "separated from the natural world", so they slept outside a lot. She used to put those breakaway collars on them, but they had lost so many that she gave up. Yin disappeared into the woodlot occasionally, but preferred to sleep on the porch. Yan spent his days stalking small flying or furry critters, but even he showed up promptly to be fed.

Until one Friday.

Jeanne was puzzled by his absence but not alarmed until the following morning, when he missed his second meal. She even knocked on Abner's door and asked him if he'd seen Yan. When he failed to show up by Saturday evening, she had become distraught. "He must have fallen into the millrace and drowned," she told Victoria. "He was too street smart to get hit by a car, and too fast and mean to let a dog kill him."

But just a few hours later, Dennis spotted Yan's oddly striped coat as he trotted down the crumbling sidewalk, headed straight for home. Out tomcatting, he figured. Jeanne had been so upset that Dennis followed in Yan's wake, intending to make sure she got the news, but Jeanne had glanced out the window at just the right time and was waiting on the porch with a bowl of food in her hand.

Dennis was never really sure exactly what happened during the next few seconds. Yan yowled menacingly and ran up the steps, momentarily out of his line of sight. Then Jeanne screeched and something clattered across the porch. He ran the rest of the way and saw his neighbor cowering back as Yan stalked forward, hissing so ferociously that it sounded artificial. Dennis stepped on a loose board, which creaked, and Yan seemed to rise into the air and turn without altering his posture. The cat's face was twisted in grotesque fury.

Ed opened the screen door to find out what the commotion was all about and Yan, apparently deciding that he was outnumbered, ran to the opposite end of the porch, leaped up onto the rail, turned back to let out one last shriek of fury, then suddenly began to shake all over. Ed let the screen door slam behind him and, as if it had been a signal, Yan closed his eyes and fell off the rail. Dennis approached the motionless body cautiously, but it was immediately obvious that Yan had hissed his last hiss.

Jeanne was crying softly while Ed tried to console her. Dennis went home to get a shovel and remove the body. On his way back, he heard Jeanne cry out again. This time the outcome was less upsetting. She was sitting in her rocking chair with Yan in her lap. Yan looked put upon but was accepting tidbits Ed had retrieved from the fallen bowl. Dennis could not understand how the cat could have been restored to life and good humor, so easily, and a glance into the side yard confirmed his skepticism.

There was a dead cat there, and it looked a lot like Yan.

"We bought the cats from the Crowleys," Ed mentioned a while later, while they were digging a shallow grave. "Maybe one of his litter mates ended up going feral."

Dennis thought that was a mighty big coincidence but he couldn't offer a better explanation.

Victoria finally worked her magic and talked Laurie into coming over for lunch. Dennis was at work, of course, but she gave him a detailed report over supper that evening. "Her husband died about a year ago in an automobile accident. They were both in research of some kind but she quit her job after the insurance company paid up. She's teaching at Brown part time and doing some work of her own. She and Chloe Wrentham knew each other at Michigan State."

"No other family?"

"There's a brother somewhere, I think. Her parents are divorced and I don't think they're close. She and her husband hadn't wanted kids; she says she's always felt uncomfortable with them and wouldn't trust herself to raise any of her own. Too busy, too wrapped up in her work. In fact, she made that point often enough that I didn't protest too much when she decided to go home. I think I was meant to take the hint."

"She and Abner would make a great pair. Have they even met yet?"

"Probably not."

This conversation came back to Dennis a few weeks later when he noticed Laurie sitting on her front porch. She wasn't alone. Somehow a handful of folding chairs had appeared and she was talking with evident animation to three young boys. He didn't know their names, but at least one looked familiar. Kids came down Myrtle to explore the woods every so often. The police tried to discourage them because the millrace could be dangerous when the water was high, and there were lots of places where you could have a pretty serious fall, but kids are kids and there was no stopping them. As long as they didn't vandalize any property coming or going, no one was likely to complain about them. Dennis had no idea what would have led them into Laurie's company.

He mentioned it to Victoria and she recalled that during one of her breaks from the book she was writing, she had seen Laurie talking to a group of boys in front of her house a few days earlier. As summer advanced into fall, both of them noticed kids playing in her yard from time to time, but then August came and went, and so did the folding chairs and the badminton net Laurie had set up. The kids disappeared as if they'd never been there.

"Do you suppose she lured them into the house and ate them?" asked Victoria one evening, twisting her face in mock horror.

"There's probably a tank of piranhas in the garage." Dennis joked about it, but when he ran into Chief Dowdell a few days later, he impulsively asked him if there'd been any missing kids in the area recently.

"Not a one. You could do me a favor and abduct a dozen or so. Make my job a lot easier."

The leaves were just starting to turn when Abner deigned to accept one of our periodic invitations to dinner. Tabitha's rapid mental decline had been dramatic; Abner's was much more gradual. He had withdrawn from a world that was too loud, too violent, too fast paced. His sole concession to the present was an internet connection, through which he bought the books that occupied most of his time. There was no television set in his living room, no newspaper arrived on his doorstep in the mornings, and he hadn't realized that Clinton was no longer President until someone stuck an Obama/Biden sign on his front lawn.

The neighbors were all watching for signs of mental confusion or poor health and they were relieved at their failure to detect anything alarming. Both Abner and his clothing were invariably clean and presentable, his general health seemed good, and while it took longer for him to assemble an appropriate conversational response than had once been the case, his remarks were appropriate and occasionally insightful.

"So how's life treating you lately, Abner?" Dennis asked. "No complaints?"

He rummaged in his pocket and withdrew his pipe. Abner didn't smoke any more – doctor's orders – but he still liked to suck on it. "Just the one."

Dennis raised an eyebrow. "Which one was that?"

"Them damned kids. Making noises in the middle of the night. It's not right."

Dennis and Victoria exchanged looks. "Which kids are you talking about, Abner?" she asked.

"The new people. You know, the ones moved in next door."

"There's just Miss Kaitan there, Abner. She's a widow and doesn't have any children."

"Not all the time, she doesn't. But every once in a while she does. I can hear them shouting and laughing and crying."

"Well, maybe she has overnight company some times," suggested Victoria, but that was unlikely. The only other vehicles they had ever seen at Laurie's house had been delivery trucks and the pickup, which had returned a few times to move items to Chloe's home, and twice in the opposite direction. The neighbors all wondered about this but only Victoria had actually tried to find out. Laurie had rebuffed her politely but firmly.

Autumn slid on by and one Monday evening in early October, Victoria had some news. "We've been invited to dinner by one of the neighbors."

"Touraine or Blackwood?"

"Neither."

I blinked. It couldn't be Abner. "Kaitan? What's the occasion?"

She gave me an exaggerated smile. "She wants us to meet her fiancé."

Darren Prescott was about thirty, his hair showing hints of gray, his belly just beginning to expand. Dennis realized after only a few minutes that he didn't like the man. At first he wasn't quite sure what it was. Prescott talked just a bit too quickly, laughed a shade louder than was called for, and stood uncomfortably close when he was speaking to someone. Dennis tried to tell himself that the young man was just nervous, but he exuded such an overpowering sense of self confidence that the explanation was unconvincing. He was wound too tight, as if he was high on drugs. Dennis even wondered if that might be the case.

"How did you and Laurie get together anyway?" Dennis was honestly interested. When had she had the opportunity to meet someone, let alone conduct a romance?

"Oh, we met through her job."

"Do you work at Brown?"

Darren hesitated, for the first time since I'd met him, and Laurie quickly intervened. "Darren is helping me with my research. He's in private industry."

"You never did say what you were working on," prompted Victoria.

"Desalinization," came the quick response. "You know, making salt water drinkable."

Her reluctance to talk about her work aside, Laurie was polite, even charming, but she was careful to stay within sight and sound of Darren. There was an underlying tension that Dennis felt more than subliminally. It was as though she was afraid that Darren would embarrass her in some way.

The evening was not entirely satisfactory. Laurie clearly wasn't interested in cultivating their acquaintance and it wasn't at all clear why she'd asked them over. Darren, on the other hand, loved to talk about the subject most important to him, and that subject was not, alas, Laurie Kaitan. Dennis never doubted that he felt affection for her, but his first love was clearly Darren Prescott. He went into great detail about the plans he was making once Laurie's hard work and genius paid off.

"We'll sell this property, of course. It's all right for the time being, mind you, but I know that I can find a more suitable place for us. And Laurie paid entirely too much for the house; I'm sure I could have convinced them to take a lower offer. I'll have to spruce the place up a bit to get back her investment. Fortunately, I'm an excellent carpenter."

There was more in that vein. Darren had cooked supper; he told them he had always dreamed of running his own restaurant. The food was palatable but unexceptional. He recommended a "recent" bestseller, which Dennis had read two years earlier, and explained that the book would have been even better if the first third had been shortened and the character of the undertaker drawn more deeply. "I've been thinking about writing a novel myself one of these days. I just haven't found the time."

Prescott was an egomaniac and a bore and Dennis felt an immense sense of relief when they were finally allowed to go home. Laurie may have loved the man, but Dennis was convinced that he'd have turned into an ax murderer within a week if he'd been forced to live with Darren Prescott.

They had walked almost all the way home before Dennis stopped and glanced back.

"What's wrong?" asked Victoria.

"Where's his car? How did he get here?"

"Maybe she picked him up somewhere. Maybe he doesn't drive because he hasn't found a car worthy of his talents."

Dennis let it go, but in bed that night he realized that it was the eve of trash day. Laurie's VW had been blocked into her driveway by a pile of refuse for at least thirty--six hours. I suppose he could have taken a cab, he told himself, and went back to sleep.

A week later, Abner disappeared. His mail overflowed the mailbox and Michelle called the police. None of the neighbors had a key to the house but they found a window that wasn't locked and got inside. There was no sign of Abner and no indication of foul play. He hadn't owned a car, so that means of tracing him was closed. The police organized a search of the nearby woodlands but nothing turned up. Officially they were still actively looking for him three days later, but the Chief told people privately that they had looked every place they could think of. No one mentioned the millrace but it was in everyone's mind. If Abner had fallen in, his body might have been carried miles downstream.

"Sometimes these older folks wander off. Usually they turn up eventually." He didn't say how often they turned up alive. There had been no indication that Abner's mind was more than mildly impaired, but there was always the possibility of a sudden onset, even a stroke. His neighbors told each other that he would be back, but none of them really believed it.

Darren Prescott, who had moved in with Laurie, was initially a hit with most of the neighbors. He went golfing with Ray Touraine and shot skeets with Ed Blackwood. Dennis invited the couple to the annual Last Barbecue of the Year Party just after Halloween, and when Darren wasn't bragging about his cooking skills or telling people how they should restructure their lives for success, he wasn't bad company. Nor was he lazy. Dennis had seen him working around their house several times and the grounds were looking considerably better than they ever had. He washed the car, cleaned out the gutters, trimmed the hedges, pruned the trees, and repaired a couple of broken windows. Dennis envied him his youthful energy. On the other hand, he didn't appear to be employed any longer. He rarely left the house and his maintenance chores left little time for him to be assisting with Laurie's research, whatever that was.

Then one Saturday Ray came home from a golf match and Michelle wasn't home, but there was a birthday cake turning to charcoal in the oven. He searched the house and yard thoroughly, then checked with the neighbors. The Blackwoods were away visiting their son's family, but Dennis was home using one of his vacation days to work on the gazebo. He had been procrastinating for months and it would soon be too cold to paint if he didn't finish it quickly.

Dennis suggested that Ray call the police. "She might have had an accident." They responded quickly and conducted a thorough search, but without finding anything helpful. The neighbors, including Prescott and Kaitan, were all questioned much more extensively this time and the police asked, firmly, if they could search the individual houses. Laurie seemed poised to refuse, but she gave in finally, and no one else objected. Dennis gave them his spare key to the Blackwoods after calling to get Ed's verbal permission to do so. There was no sign of Michelle.

Ray was alternately inconsolable and upbeat. "She'll be home any time now," he'd say, and then a few minutes later, "How will I get along without her?"

His friends were all worried about him but couldn't think of anything to do. His daughter came and stayed for a few days, and their son was there for a weekend. Then, a couple of weeks into November, I found a typed note in my mailbox.

Dear Ted and Sheri,

I'm going away for a while to think things over. I've called a taxi to take me to the airport. I need to be alone for a while. Will talk to you after the holidays.

His name was typed, not signed, at the bottom. Ray Touraine couldn't type and they didn't even own a typewriter. Dennis thought about it for a while and then called Chief Dowdell.

If anything the questions were more pointed and the searching more intense. Everyone agreed to let the police tramp through their houses again and even Laurie Kaitan volunteered without prompting. A forensics specialist took the letter and envelope away and two more went through the Touraine house looking for clues. If they found anything it was never made public. *C.S.I.* might look good on television, but in real life, it's not that easy.

Chief Dowdell increased the frequency of patrols in the area, but it was a gesture rather than a comfort. Myrtle Lane had lost a third of its residents in less than four months, and that lonely corner of Managansett was suddenly looking even lonelier. Jeanne Blackwood talked openly about moving away, and the Scoggins were thinking along similar lines.

Thanksgiving was a somber affair. The Blackwoods were away again, and Dennis had balked when Victoria suggested having Darren and Laurie over, so for the first time in a decade, they had turkey by themselves. He had the following Friday off, so when Victoria went shopping Dennis decided to clear away the last of the trash from the gazebo, now painted and rather spiffy looking, if he did say so himself. There was a pile of broken and leftover boards, including several salvaged from Laurie's trash, and he wanted to stack them neatly with the firewood. He was about half done when he picked up a nasty splinter and paused to suck at the wound, glaring at the offending board.

Stenciled on one side was a company name. Darren & Prescott. Alarm bells started ringing inside his head. Dennis decided that a call to Chief Dowdell might be in order, but he never made it to the house. He was halfway there when someone came rushing out of the bushes, swinging something long and dark, and then there was an instant of blinding pain and sudden terror before the blackness.

Dennis woke in a poorly lit room. His arms were tied behind his back and his ankles were bound together and to a large metal cabinet, too heavy to topple or move. The floor was cement, the walls were unfinished wood, and there were no windows, just an emergency light in one corner. It was almost certainly a garage. Several very large shapes loomed on either side, like oversized furniture, but he couldn't see clearly enough to identify them.

Dennis realized suddenly that he was not alone. Someone else lay a few feet away, bound in similar fashion, someone with long hair and a slightly built body. For one horrid second he feared that it was Victoria, but then he noticed the hair color was wrong. It was a bit longer before he realized his companion in ropes was Laurie Kaitan, and that suggested that it was her garage.

"Laurie? Is that you?" Dennis spoke in a whisper, wary of making his return to awareness more public. Laurie didn't answer at first and he started working on the ropes, trying to get his wrists free. It hurt like the devil and he had to stop every minute or two and let the pain wash away. During one of those pauses, Laurie groaned and started moving around. Dennis called her name again and this time she responded.

"Are you all right?"

"For now, yes." She didn't sound enthusiastic.

"Can you move toward me?"

Squirming sounds. "Not really. My wrists are tied to the gas meter."

"Did you see who did this?" Dennis was pretty sure he knew, and she confirmed it, after a fashion.

"It was Dean, of course. Darren, I mean. Oh hell, what's the point? His real name was...is Dean. Dean Kaitan."

Even bound hand and foot and waiting for the return of a presumed murderer, Dennis was intrigued and asked her what was going on. He did have the sense to resume his escape attempt while listening, although there were times when she said things so bizarre that he was momentarily stunned.

Laurie had been working on a project with Chloe Wrentham, developing some discovery of her late uncle. Chloe had found his journals and understood enough to realize she had stumbled onto something that could make her very rich, but she didn't have the technological background necessary to develop it. So Chloe had looked up her old friend, told her just enough to whet her appetite, and Laurie had moved to Managansett. Carl Wrentham's experiments had been only partially successful and Laurie had suggested that the problem was with his equipment and not his theory. The two of them had financed an upgrade and were making progress when Laurie's estranged husband, Dean, showed up. Dean had disappeared a year earlier after embezzling money from a real estate brokerage house and had been hiding from the police ever since. Somehow he had tracked down Laurie and – at least so she claimed – she had been afraid to turn him in because the scandal might jeopardize her position at Brown. Dennis suspected that the truth was that Darren would implicate her in the embezzlement. She wasn't making enough money as an adjunct professor to buy a house and expensive sophisticated scientific equipment.

"Carl found a way to replicate physical objects. He couldn't make gold out of dirt or anything like that, but if he had enough of the raw materials, he could create a duplicate of a piece of jewelry in seconds."

The process worked on living organisms as well, she said, but only physiologically. There had been no transfer of personality or intelligence, and the duplicate bodies ceased to function in a matter of hours. "Chloe and I didn't care about that, not at first. We just wanted to make enough money to finance things until we found a way to go public. If we could make carbon into diamonds, our resource problem would be solved. But there was some kind of glitch in Carl's design. The copies weren't exact. The diamonds might look identical to the naked eye, but they were invariably flawed. There were other inconsistencies, and we assumed that this also explained the failures with living creatures."

Dennis was beginning to tire and he didn't think the ropes were any looser than they had been. "So how does that lead to us being tied up in your garage?"

She sighed. "The process works by scanning the original and then configuring the copy. It doesn't have to be completed immediately; we can store the scan indefinitely. I was convinced that the scans were fine, but that the resolution in the configuration chamber wasn't precise enough. We worked on that premise and the results suggested that the answer was more complex than that. Higher resolution eliminated the errors we were used to, but others showed up. My diamond ring had no internal flaws, but it was milky, almost opaque. When Dean showed up, he suggested we might learn something using live subjects again, and even made a copy of himself. It lived for three days and seemed to be intermittently aware of us. Then, a couple of weeks ago, Dean had an accident." Her voice wavered and Dennis told himself she was about to lie to him. "He fell down the basement stairs at Chloe's place and broke his neck."

"He looks pretty much alive to me," Dennis said sarcastically, but he already had a presentiment of what she was about to tell him.

"After I moved here, I continued working on the resolution. I lured a cat into the house and put a bowl of cream in the scanning chamber. The copy looked perfect and, for the first time, it seemed to be fully conscious. A little too conscious. It scratched my arm when I opened the chamber door and escaped through an open window before I could catch it."

Yan, Dennis thought. Or his deceased twin brother.

"I tried other subjects – mice, insects, a parakeet, goldfish. Eventually they stopped dying, but I noticed several cases of bizarre behavior. At first I thought it was just heightened aggression, but later I concluded it's more subtle than that. The resolution process simplifies and emphasizes attributes. A bad tempered animal becomes even more so; another prone to panic attacks dies of fear. Some of the boys couldn't stop crying, or giggling, and one of them even attacked me."

Dennis remembered Abner's complaints about the sound of children next door and wondered what had happened to them – the duplicates. "You made another copy of your husband."

"I loved him! I still love him!" Her voice broke. "I had to bring him back!"

They were silent for a time. Dennis was working at his bonds again and he'd chafed most of the skin off his wrists. "He was a vain man, wasn't he?"

She laughed, but it was hysteria, not humor. "Yes, he was. Dean always thought he was destined for greatness, even though I suppose objectively that he was unexceptional. I didn't mind, because I knew he loved me almost as much as he loved himself."

"But not any more."

"That's not Dean. That's Darren. They're all Darren."

Dennis blinked. "Come again?"

"I kept trying to adjust the scan. It took four more tries before I got a Darren who wouldn't die within a day or so. This particular Darren wanted to get the work done faster, and he wanted to impress the neighbors, and there wasn't enough time to do it all. So he decided to recruit some help. And what better help could there be than another of himself? We didn't have all the materials so he went out and harvested some. I had no idea what he was doing until two of them came to supper that evening."

Dennis was doing a lot of blinking. "You said harvesting. Does that mean what I think it means?"

She sobbed softly and didn't answer right away. "I didn't know about it until afterwards, I swear. I never hurt any of the kids. Not the originals. And their copies all just stopped living."

"He killed Abner?"

"Yes. He was the second."

It was cold but Dennis was sweating. His voice came out flat and deliberate. "The second?"

"Darren blamed Chloe for his…accident. When I brought him back, he seemed perfectly all right, but that night he got out of bed, said he was restless, went for a walk. He was gone about an hour. When I called Chloe the next day, there was no answer. I went over -- I have my own key – and there was no sign of her. But when I checked the equipment, I could tell that a lot of raw material had been added since the previous day. One hundred and twenty pounds in fact. I didn't know what to do so I've been taking in her mail and paying her bills ever since."

Dennis shivered, and not because he was cold.

"After that Darren loafed around while the other Darren was out working in the yard, but the second one didn't think it was fair for him to do all the heavy work, so the two of them decided to make a third."

"That would be when he took Michelle?"

"Yes." It was a whisper.

"And then Raymond?"

"They needed a fourth for bridge. Dean loved the game but I never learned to play."

"So why am I here? Is Darren taking up basketball next? And why are you tied up?"

"Dean always enjoyed sex and so do the Darrens, naturally. But with four of them and only one of me, they're getting a little frustrated. So they told me they wanted to make a duplicate, that it would be easier for me that way. I refused, they insisted, I made threats, and they restrained me. They're going to duplicate me tonight. If I'm right, if the process untangles conflicting personality traits and makes them more pronounced, the other me will object even more than I do, but they're convinced they can talk us both into it eventually."

"Okay, that's why you're here. So why…" His thoughts answered his question, but she said them out loud.

"You're the raw materials."

"So what happens? Do I just dissolve when the new you appears?"

"No, the elements in your body have to be stored in a tank like the one we've installed in Chloe's basement." She nodded toward a looming, squarish shape. It's a little bigger than that one. "They'll take us over there after dark."

Dennis squinted at it. "It would have to be a lot bigger than that."

"It's not. They'll have to cut you up first."

Suddenly his wrists didn't hurt nearly as bad as they had a moment before. He went back to work on the ropes. An image slipped into his mind, of Laurie with a butcher knife, chopping up the bodies of duplicated young boys, and his stomach churned.

In a movie, Dennis would have freed himself and Laurie, found a shovel or something to use as a weapon, brained the first

Darren to enter the laboratory, then called the police and lived happily ever after. It didn't go quite like that.

They heard raised voices from inside the house, but couldn't tell what was being said. It sounded like an argument. That went on for quite a while, increasing and decreasing in volume. Then it got much louder and there were other noises, breaking glass, thumps and bumps and bangs, a high pitched cry that might have been a scream, grunts and groans and shouts of anger. There was obviously trouble in paradise. It lasted for almost an hour, although it seemed much longer to the two prisoners. Then it slowly began to diminish and eventually died out completely.

Dennis still hadn't managed to get his hands free and the ropes were now sticky and wet with sweat and blood. He was exhausted and his arms had cramped so badly that he was unable to continue struggling. Laurie had sobbed for a while, then became silent and wouldn't even respond when he spoke to her.

But when the door finally opened and the lights came on, Dennis realized that he still desperately wanted to live.

He turned his head, trying to think of something biting and heroic to say to Darren before he was chopped into cutlets, but it wasn't Darren in the doorway. It was a uniformed officer with weapon drawn.

It was Victoria who had saved the day. When she came home and found her husband missing without having left a note behind, she immediately called Chief Dowdell. The searchers had found Laurie's door closed but unlocked. No one responded to the bell, but one of the officers shined his light through a window and saw Darren lying dead on the kitchen floor. That was just about the same time that another officer looked in through the living room window and saw Darren lying dead on the couch.

There was another one in the hallway, and the fourth was on the stairs. Three of them were dead and the fourth died a few hours later. One had a caved in skull, one had bled to death from stab wounds, the third had his throat torn out, and the last survivor had multiple ruptured internal organs. There was a lot of blood. There was also a crowd of very confused police officers. It was impossible to reconstruct just what had happened but Dennis was satisfied with his own theory, which he shared only with Victoria. There had been four supercharged egos who had already casually killed three people and who all wanted to be at the top of the pecking order. It wouldn't have taken much to have them at each other's throats, and better their jugulars than his.

There was no evidence linking Laurie to the disappearances and she was clearly not involved in the deaths of her husbands. She never mentioned the duplication equipment until Dennis started to allude to it, then laughed and insisted that she had made the entire story up. Chief Dowdell wasn't particularly imaginative and he didn't like puzzles; the mystery of four identical corpses was bothersome so he just ignored it and pretty soon so did everyone else.

Chloe Wrentham's disappearance didn't make much more than a ripple. She had made no friends in town and would not be dismissed.

Victoria would not let Dennis out of her sight for weeks afterwards and he finally protested that he wasn't a child to be watched over.

"I just can't get enough of you," she said.

"Be careful what you wish for," said Dennis.

Part III: MISPRINTS

I was actually in a pretty good mood the night the dead woman tried to run me down. We had just wrapped up the Randall case with some nice photographs of the subject hauling cinderblocks around his backyard, snapped by one of my stringers who had climbed up into a neighbor's tree to peer over Randall's stockade fence.

I'd had dinner in Providence with some friends, but they'd parked at the mall garage and I was way up at the other end of town in a private lot I knew no one monitored at night, so we said our goodbyes and went our separate ways. There was a fair amount of traffic in the city proper, but it thinned as I got further out. The sky was so clear it looked fake and I was enjoying the chance to move around. Unlike television detectives, I spend most of my time sitting at a desk, staring at a computer screen. I felt more like an accountant than a private investigator. During my twenty year career I'd never been shot at or knocked unconscious, I was on good terms with the local police, and I'd never once called all the suspects together to reveal my solution to a mystery. The closest I'd ever come to drama was the time I was made by a philandering husband who screamed at me and followed me all the way back to my car, threatening to shove my camera down my throat.

I turned into Baker Street, which wasn't much more than an alley. It was brightly lit for its entire length and I'd never felt nervous using it to shave a few steps off my route. In retrospect, I'm not even sure that I noticed the SUV parked at the far end, at least not before the headlights blinked on, and I didn't pay much attention even then. The driver raced the engine and I figured it was just some kids from one of the dance clubs two blocks over, and it was the possibility that they might be drunk and inattentive that prompted me to look around rather than any actual premonition of danger. There were narrow sidewalks on both sides of the street, but no doorways or alcoves, just a small dumpster under one window with a billowing, makeshift chute above it. Renovations of some kind.

The engine really began to race and I picked up my pace, hoping to get past before they started moving, but then I heard screeching rubber and it was coming toward me, and that's when I started to get scared. The SUV lunged like some predator sighting its prey. If I hadn't had the presence of mind to jump forward instead of back, I would have been smeared all over the nearest wall. As it was, the side view mirror clipped my arm as we passed each other, spinning me around. I stumbled but managed to keep my balance, wondering what the hell was going on.

The SUV scraped along the side of the building, then lurched back into the middle of the alley and came to a stop. I was about to shout something obscene when it started moving again, this time in reverse. The driver wasn't in complete control and I avoided it easily, then headed toward the dumpster. There was another minor collision behind me, but by then I was running full out. I felt like a toreador escaping an enraged bull as I pulled myself up the side of the dumpster, banging one knee painfully in the process. Then there was a bang as big as the world and everything seemed to move, but I held on, pulled myself higher, and glanced back down.

The SUV had struck the dumpster at an angle, turning it part way into the street. The engine was racing again and the wheels spinning like crazy. I thought at first the driver was trying to push the dumpster forward, but then realized the truth. The passenger side front quarter was twisted and torn and had cut into the tire. The driver must have realized that the SUV was effectively out of commission because she – that's right, she – stepped out of the car. If the woman had been armed, it would have been all over then, because my own weapon hadn't been out of the safe in my office for at least six months. She gave me a look of cold fury and turned away, running up the alley toward Westminster Street.

Why didn't I chase her? Well, for one thing my knee hurt and for another, I work at a desk most of the time and I'm out of shape. But the truth was, I'd recognized her, and that recognition had stunned me. Her name was Laurie Carter and she was dead and I was responsible for her death, sort of.

I called the police and they came, eventually, looked the SUV over – it had been stolen earlier that day – and took my statement. Detective Williams looked doubtful when I said it had been deliberate, not an accident. He promised to get back to me but admitted they weren't hopeful. I'd given them a description, of course, but decided not to provide her name. It's hard to get the police to take you seriously when you suggest you've been attacked by ghosts or zombies; hell, it's hard to get them to take you seriously when you don't.

They dropped me off at my car when I refused medical treatment and I drove home very tentatively, watching the rear view mirror constantly, half expecting some other kamikaze vehicle to come flying in my direction. But nothing happened, I reached the house safely, and I was very careful to set the alarms before going to bed.

I was at the office early the following morning and as soon as I came in I told Jeannie, my receptionist, to get me the Carter file. And before you ask, Jeannie has three grandchildren and varicose veins, not sleek gams. She does have a sexy telephone voice though.

At my desk, I paged through the Carter documentation. It was a pretty routine divorce case, right up until the end. Ted and Laurie Carter were both fast track yuppies. He worked in biotechnology and had been promoted out of the labs and into administration by the time he was thirty. Laurie was an electronics whiz, headed her own team for a mid-sized company that did a lot of classified government work. That had been a bit of a headache because it made it a lot harder to get a handle on what she was up to inside the compound, which was surrounded by formidable security fences and monitored 24/7. She had a pretty good sized lab at home as well. The Carters had bought one of those fake farmhouse and barn combinations, and the latter was her private electronics playhouse.

Anyway, Ted Carter had hired us to conduct surveillance on his wife. He was pretty sure, he claimed, that she was seeing another man. The high security at her workplace was a problem. So was the relative isolation of their home. I couldn't very well park a surveillance van on the street in front of their property for days on end without arousing suspicion. With the husband's assistance, I installed a tap and record device on their telephone line, but she had a cell phone so I wasn't hopeful and we never did get anything useful from it. I'm no psychologist, but while I was in her bedroom installing the tap, I couldn't help noticing that she had lots of framed photographs on the walls. All of them were pictures of herself. She also had four mirrors, not counting the one in the bathroom. This woman, I concluded, is in love with herself, not her husband.

Carter got suspicious when she started spending more time working in her home laboratory and less at the main plant. She had also become diffident about sex, was frequently distracted, and increasingly irritable. A chance encounter with one of his wife's co-workers had revealed that Laurie had been taking sick and vacation days with increasing frequency and that there was concern that she was concealing some serious medical condition.

Carter told me he wanted to know the truth, but like most people in his situation, what he really wanted was to be told that everything was all right, that Laurie was just suffering from overwork. It was her second marriage – her first husband, Dean Kaitan, had died under mysterious circumstances - but his first. I explained the difficulties to him, which he interpreted as an attempt to inflate my charges, to which I might have taken offense except that almost all of my clients feel that I inflate my charges. I don't. If I wasn't competitive, I wouldn't stay in business. He finally agreed and I assigned the Bobbsey Twins – that's Bob Anderson and Bob Bergstrom – to the job.

A week later, I thought we might catch a break. Thanks to the phone tap I knew that Laurie was taking an extended leave of absence from work – without pay. She told her husband that she was developing a project of her own with "stupendous potential".

The rest of the story is pretty sordid. She was meeting her lover in the laboratory almost every day after that. It was another woman. We never did catch the lover coming or going, and I had long wondered how she managed that. But we had some tapes of their pillow talk, and a not very artistic but reasonably explicit bit of film taken by a camera mounted in the loft that showed Laurie Carter in a variety of compromising positions. We never did find out who the second woman was. She managed to keep her face off camera despite their enthusiastic bed play.

I delivered the audiotapes and a CD with the camera footage to Carter, who confronted his wife with them that very evening. Laurie Carter fell down a staircase a few hours later and broke her neck. Her husband claimed that when he confronted her with the evidence, she'd alternated between begging him to forgive her and berating him for spying on her, that she'd eventually attacked him and that they'd both fallen from the landing. He even had a dislocated shoulder and assorted bangs and bruises as corroboration. There was talk of a murder charge, but either he convinced the police he was telling the truth, or they decided they lacked sufficient evidence to convict. I was inclined to think he was guilty, but he was my client and I kept my mouth shut.

Somewhere in there I got paid, but only after I tracked Carter down. He'd been asked to resign from his job by then, but the insurance company had been forced to settle, and he and his wife had some serious investments. Carter had closed up the house and gone to Europe for an extensive "period of healing" without having paid my final bill.

I called his house and got an answering machine, which at least meant he was back in town. Then I opened the safe and found my handgun, buried under a stack of contracts.

Carter's house looked pretty much the same as the last time I'd seen it. The grass had been cut recently, but it badly needed raking. There was a BMW parked out front. I rang the doorbell and after a few seconds the door swung open. It was Ted Carter, all right, but he'd colored his hair and swapped glasses for contacts. Trying for the younger look, I imagine, now that he was single again. He didn't look pleased to see me.

"What do you want, Burton?"

Philip Marlowe would have grabbed him by the shirt front but I dropped my eyes and spoke as pleasantly as I could manage. Challenging the belligerent witness might feel good emotionally but it's rarely productive. "I just wanted to stop by and see how you were doing, Mr. Carter."

"I'm doing just fine, and I'm only going to be here long enough to arrange for the sale of this place." The door started to close.

"I'm very sorry that things worked out the way they did. I never felt as though we really finished the job you hired us for."

That was enough to get the door reopened, but not enough for an invitation to come in. "What do you mean?" His voice wasn't quite as antagonistic. Maybe he thought I had come to offer him a partial refund.

"We never did find out the name of your wife's…friend." I hurried past that point, not wishing to give his anger a chance to rekindle. "I guess if it were me, I'd feel like I'd been left…hanging." I tried to mime that I was at a loss for words.

"No closure," he offered helpfully.

"Right. So I thought I might take another look around, maybe come up with a name, or a reason. Something." His eyes narrowed so I added hastily that there would, of course, be no further charge. "Professional pride," I told him.

I still didn't get invited in, but he didn't set the metaphorical dogs on me either. There was nothing of Laurie's left in the house, he told me. "I gave it all away or put it in the trash. You're wasting your time. She was too paranoid and unstable to leave anything incriminating lying around."

I bit my lip. "What about her lab?" My eyes moved to the barn.

He glanced that way as well, as though surprised to see that it was still there. "I haven't gotten around to that yet. I don't like going in there. That's where they were together…" Carter let his voice trail off, trying to look despondent, failing abysmally. The only place he was hurting was his pride.

"Would it be possible for me to take a look around? I might find something that we missed."

"I'll have to find the key." After that, it was impossible for him to avoid letting me inside. I stood in his living room – the furniture was all covered with sheets so there was no place to sit – until he returned. "Here it is. I'll want that back when you go."

"Sure. One more thing. Did your wife have a sister, Mr. Carter?"

He frowned. "No, she was an only child. Her mother was killed when she was an infant and as far as I know her father never remarried. They weren't close."

I hadn't visited the barn personally before now, although I'd reviewed the pictures. The narrow focus of the camera hadn't done it justice. It felt bigger on the inside than on the outside, with high vaulted ceilings, a loft that extended three quarters of the way around the perimeter but which left a very large open space in the center.

The ground floor was full of electronic equipment, almost none of which I could identify. There were units on benches and tables, and others freestanding on the floor. There were two glass walled enclosures so large that I could stand inside and raise both arms without touching anything, and a third, considerably smaller. Ropes of cable snaked across the floor and disappeared into huge junction boxes mounted on the walls. A switch inside the door turned on a bank of fluorescent lights.

At the rear of the building someone had installed a poorly equipped kitchen and a small bathroom. I opened the refrigerator and glanced inside, did the same for some of the cupboards, poked my head into the bathroom, then seated myself on the sofa, glancing up unconsciously to where one of the Bobbsey Twins had installed the camera that caught Laurie and her girlfriend in mid-tryst. I was pretty certain that I was alone in the building, but I touched my weapon briefly, just to be sure it was really there. The refrigerator was well stocked, there were fresh towels in the bath, and I could faintly smell the last meal cooked here. Lamb. It was too fresh to be left over from before Laurie Carter's death. And most of the equipment I'd seen had been free of dust. The couch on which I was sitting was a convertible bed, and there were blankets and pillows sitting in a corner.

Someone had been living here while Ted Carter was off dealing with his bruised ego. Could it be the same someone who had tried to kill me the night before? Could it be Laurie Carter's unidentified lover? Was it possible that the two women had looked a great deal alike, so much so that after Laurie's death, her partner reinforced those similarities so well that I hadn't been able to tell the difference? I had seen her in poor light, under great stress, and for only a few seconds. It wouldn't have been hard to pull off the masquerade under those circumstances.

It worked for me, but I couldn't see myself suggesting that scenario to Detective Martinelli of the Providence Police Department. Too Hollywood.

After a while I stood up, intending to return to the main house, but then I had a stroke of luck. There was a set of keys on one of the benches, and when I went through them, I found a duplicate of the one Carter had loaned me. I pocketed it, took a last look around, turned off the lights and locked the door behind me.

"Find anything or are you just wasting my time?" Carter was mad at me again.

"Nothing definite. I'll be in touch."

There was a small crisis at the office when I got back. Wilder had blown his cover and had actually been assaulted by the subject he was surveilling. No serious physical damage, but we'd have to back off and find another approach on that case. Then a process server subpoenaed me in the Trachtman litigation; I'd hoped that our documentation would speak for itself. By the time everything was sorted out, I was tired, it was dark outside, and I'd managed to stop thinking about Laurie Carter.

But someone else hadn't stopped thinking about me.

I parked in the driveway, walked down to the mailbox at the curb and retrieved my mail, slipping it into my jacket pocket. I was on the porch steps when I heard something, a slight rustle in the shrubs despite the dead calm of the air. It might have been a neighbor's cat or a skunk out for a nocturnal stroll, but my nerves were still on edge. I froze where I was and, very slowly, unsnapped my shoulder holster and drew my weapon, holding it down at my side. My hands were shaking and I was suddenly sweating despite the cool breeze.

Just as I was about to relax and tell myself that I was nuts, the shrubs moved more violently and a figure stepped out into the moonlight. Although I couldn't see her clearly, I was sure this was the same person who had tried to run me down a day earlier. I used my thumb to release the safety as she took another step forward, raising her arm. I knew with absolute certainty that she was carrying a weapon this time.

"Goodbye, Mr. Burton," she said suddenly.

"One question…" I blurted out quickly and she hesitated. I didn't. My weapon came up and I fired three times, the shots seeming abnormally loud. She fired once, but probably by reflex. At that range I couldn't have missed but she did. The woman seemed to rise up onto her toes, then flew backward, landing flat on her back.

Still holding my weapon ready, I approached cautiously. There was a .38 lying beside one hand and I kicked that into the bushes. Then I crouched and felt for a pulse. Nothing. There were at least two pools of darkness spreading across the front of her torso.

She was dressed in a blouse and slacks and had her hair tied up in a bun. One of my neighbors had turned his lights on but no one came outside. I needed the police and, naturally, my cell phone battery was dead. So I went inside and called from the kitchen. I suppose I was in shock because I did what needed to be done mechanically, not wanting to deal with the fact that I'd just taken a human life.

It took a while to convince them I wasn't kidding, that I'd just killed an armed assailant, and it took a bit longer before a prowl car showed up. By then I'd turned on the outside lights but I was back in the house. I'd planned to wait for them beside the body, but the body was gone. I was quite sure that I'd killed the woman and that she hadn't walked off by herself, but I wasn't quite as sure that her confederate wasn't still around.

The police were a bit less skeptical this time, particularly after I found the discarded .38 and pointed out the blood stains, and they made me come to the station to make my statement. I told them my suspicions of a connection to the Carter case and it was duly noted.

I didn't get home until well past the witching hour so I slept in late the next morning. When I finally got up, I called the office to tell them I wouldn't be in; it's good to be the boss. Then I called Ted Carter's house, but got no answer. There was still crime scene tape on the front lawn, but it had rained during the night and all traces of blood had been washed away.

I drove past the Carter place without stopping. The BMW was still in the driveway. At the next corner I made a turn and parked in a little picnic area, then started walking back, cutting through a small apple orchard and approaching from a sheltered side of the house. I scouted the grounds as best I could and peeked in some windows, but there were no signs of life. The barn had no windows on the ground floor, which meant that I couldn't look in, but which also meant that anyone inside would be unable to look out and see me coming.

I rang the bell at the house and knocked a few times, but there was no response. Then I took a deep breath and started toward the barn, not sure if I was actually going to illegally enter or not. When I saw splotches of blood on the threshold, the decision was made for me.

With one hand clutching my weapon, I unlocked the door. The lights were on, and I'd turned them off. There was no inner sanctum creak as I eased the door open, but I doubt that I could have entered without alerting anyone inside. As it happened, the two people who waited for me were both past the point of caring.

There was a relatively clear space in one corner of the laboratory, and someone had spread a tarp on the floor. I was pretty sure it hadn't been there during my first visit. I was absolutely positive that the two dead bodies hadn't been on top of it. One of them was Ted Carter, looking very surprised as he lay on his back with a bloody hole in the center of his forehead. Beside him was a slightly built woman with two gory bullet wounds in her chest, presumably the very same wounds I'd inflicted the previous evening. I crouched and stared at her face very closely. I hadn't seen Laurie Carter for a year, but if this woman wasn't her twin sister, I'd have been very much surprised.

I reached for my cell phone, then remembered that it was sitting on my night table, recharging.

If I'd had any brains, I'd have run from that place and called the police from a neighbor's house. Curiosity got the better of me, though, and I finished exploring. I confirmed that I was the only – living – person inside, but I did make another interesting discovery. The card table in the kitchen still had dirty dishes on it. There were three places set. The dead woman, her unknown confederate, and Ted Carter? That seemed possible. Good old Ted might somehow have been coaxed into collaborating with the murderous duo. But there were traces of bacon and eggs on the plates, and they looked relatively fresh. The woman I'd shot certainly hadn't eaten anything this morning, and while I have very little experience with dead bodies, it looked to me as though Ted had died more than a few hours ago. The blood was completely dry and he looked very pale, as though all the blood had succumbed to the pull of gravity.

So what was I dealing with here?

I sat thoughtfully for so long that I nearly got caught without a struggle. It was actually a few seconds after I heard the car drive up and the engine stop that I realized my danger. I started toward the door, heard voices beyond it, and hastily retreated. There was a spiral staircase leading up to the loft, which was used mostly for storage, and I climbed it as quickly as I could, then hid behind a stack of cardboard cartons. I had barely gotten settled when the door opened.

Three figures entered. They were talking softly, and I only caught occasional words, not enough to provide any meaning. I strained to get a better view. One of the oversized glass chambers was obstructing my vision. I almost gave myself away a few moments later by gasping when the first of the figures came close enough for me to recognize her.

She was a dead ringer for Laurie Carter. You're probably ahead of me by now, but I'll say it anyway. Her two companions became visible a few seconds later. They were also versions of Laurie Carter. They were dressed differently, and one had her hair braided and one had a ponytail and one had let her hair fall loosely, but they all had the same face, the same build, the same voice, and the same mannerisms. They were all Laurie Carter.

A little time passed. I'm not sure exactly how much because what I had just seen required some fairly intensive mental processing and I think my consciousness was effectively offline for at least a few seconds. What recalled me to my situation was hearing my name mentioned. I strained to hear, and caught much of what followed, because two of the women were now directly beneath me, doing something enigmatic, one at a keyboard, the other turning knobs on another mysterious piece of electronic equipment. The third was out of sight and they had raised their voices to include her in their conversation.

They didn't like me very much. There was quite a bit about how low subhuman private investigators in general and Paul Burton in particular would stoop. My vanity prevents me from providing the particulars, but suffice it to say that they held me responsible for the death of their "sister." At no time did they refer to each other by name and the only way I could differentiate among them was by dubbing them Ponytail, Braids, and Windblown. Windblown was the one I couldn't see; I think she was somewhere behind the glass tanks.

Quite a bit of the equipment came on line during the next few minutes, some with a hum, some with cascading lights, some silently. Ponytail and Braids seemed to have completed what they were doing, because they walked out of my line of sight. I shifted position slightly and found them again as they were lifting the body of the woman I'd shot and killed. I don't need to give her a nickname because she wasn't around for much longer. They half carried, half dragged her to the smallest of the glass enclosures and put her inside. Once the doors were closed, Braids pressed her palm against a large, round button, a motor engaged, and I didn't see most of what happened after that. I didn't see it because I closed my eyes and turned away. The enclosure was a kind of oversized blender and the sounds that reached my hiding place made my stomach churn.

That ended after a while and I managed to look down again. A dark, thick fluid was being pumped into a series of tanks suspended over one of the two larger glass chambers. The third chamber had been opened, and Windblown was standing inside it with her arms flat against her sides, motionless. Laurie Carter was a very attractive woman and this version of her was now completely naked, but I didn't feel even a twinge of desire.

My attention was drawn to the third chamber, which was now almost opaque. The contents of the overhead tanks were being sprayed evenly throughout the interior, a fine mist that was constantly renewed. As fluid settled into the floor, it was collected in drains and recycled. Ponytail looked at some gauges and shouted something about a shortfall. She and Braids then retrieved the body of Ted Carter, dragging him to the blender. This time I looked away before they started the motor.

By the time I mustered the courage to look again, it was obvious that something strange was happening. The murky chamber seemed darker now, and as I squinted and tried to focus my eyes, I realized that a shape was taking form within the mist. I think it must have taken the better part of an hour because my legs were cramped by the time they started shutting down the equipment, but by then I'd pretty much figured out what was happening. When they opened the glass door and a fourth Laurie Carter stepped out, I wasn't even surprised.

I have to backtrack slightly now, because there's something I haven't told you, something that I noticed early on. Ponytail's speech sounded normal most of the time, but she occasionally lapsed into nonsense. Whenever this happened, she'd pause a few seconds, then resume speaking normally. Braids spoke mostly in monosyllables and very short sentences or fragments, and sometimes she took a long time before answering. Windblown didn't have either of those problems, but she would suddenly start laughing or weeping for a few seconds, for no apparent reason. Their newest sister looked exactly the same as the others, but to their consternation, she seemed completely incapable of speech.

There was obviously a flaw in the process. Laurie Carter had found a way to create copies of living beings, but they weren't exact copies. Assuming that the original Laurie Carter had died a year ago, what I was seeing now was copies, and copies of copies, and the flaws were being compounded by each replication.

After they'd found clothing for Mute, who dressed herself awkwardly, they all ate a meal while almost directly above them my treacherous stomach rumbled so loud I was afraid it would give me away. After they had cleaned up, Ponytail and Braid left. The sofa bed would only hold two, so I assumed they were going to sleep in the main house.

The lights went off and after another half hour, everything was quiet down below. I considered waiting until morning to sneak out, but I had no guarantee that they wouldn't leave one of their number behind and, frankly, the idea of spending an entire night in that chamber of horrors threatened to make me physically ill. I let another hour go by, then, weapon in hand, I very slowly descended the staircase, which was blessedly solid and silent. I could hear the sound of regular breathing from behind me, but I didn't look in that direction, afraid that even glancing at them would somehow wake one or both.

I had a tiny flashlight on my keychain and I used that to make my way to the door. I was just reaching for the handle when all the lights went on.

To this day I don't know what woke them up. I turned to find Windblown and the Mute staring at me from across the laboratory. Neither of them appeared to be armed, but that didn't stop the Mute, whose eyes blazed with hate. She began to run toward me with her hands clawed and I raised my weapon instinctively. I may have shouted something, but it wasn't a warning. There was never any doubt in my mind that I had to shoot, and I did, twice. She continued to rush forward but it was momentum now. She crashed to the floor just out of reach and never moved again.

I almost blew it then. I stood frozen. I'd killed two people in as many days and I'm no Sam Spade. I couldn't just shrug it off even if it had been self defense. I was staring down at Mute's body when Windblown came at me, swinging some long metal tool I couldn't identify. I managed to fire at her twice before it hit me on the shoulder, but I missed both times and when my arm went numb, I dropped the gun.

She saw it fall and lunged toward it, so I wrapped my good arm around her and pulled her away. Laurie had been a small woman, thank heaven, but Windblown twisted in my grasp and hit me on the bridge of the nose with the palm of one hand. It hurts just thinking about it and I released her, staggering back. Self preservation trumped pain and before she could bring the gun to bear I kicked out hard, catching her under the chin. She fell backward, fired two rounds into the ceiling before crashing down on her back.

I threw myself forward, hoping to trap her under my greater weight and wrestle the gun away, but she twisted her arm between us and I felt sudden panic. Without relinquishing my grip, I rolled to one side, pulling her along with me, and somehow in the process two more shots were fired. One of them hit the floor and shards of concrete ripped through my shirt. The other found a softer target. I felt her suddenly relax beneath me and stop struggling, and watched as her eyes rolled upward and she stopped breathing.

Without retrieving my weapon, I stood up and turned toward the door just in time to hear someone inserting a key. Braid and Ponytail must have been roused by the noise we'd made. I retreated hastily and hid behind a metal cabinet just as the door opened.

The two duplicates regarded the carnage with equanimity. I guess life is cheap when you can make some more of yourself whenever you feel like it. Braids sounded more indignant than heartbroken and Ponytail just shook her head as she picked up my weapon, looked at it blankly for a few seconds, then set it on a small table. I couldn't understand why they weren't looking for me until Braids said something about having known that "there was something wrong with the new sister". They had decided that Mute and Windblown had killed each other. Clearly the mental deterioration of the copies was more pronounced than I had realized. They decided to wait until morning to reprocess the bodies and left them lying in growing pools of blood.

I waited until they were gone, reclaimed my weapon, then gathered everything flammable I could find and piled it up in the center of the room. There was no way I could allow the survivors to create more duplicates in the morning. The fire wasn't visible when I entered the orchard, heading back to my car, but when I drove past a few minutes later, fingers of flame were leaping out of the loft windows.

There's not much more to the story. I called in an anonymous tip to the police, who found an abandoned house and a burnt out barn. There were the remains of two bodies in the ashes, and I imagine the DNA analysis caused considerable consternation because we never heard anything further about it and the bodies were never officially identified. I'm not sure what happened to Braids and Ponytail. Maybe the mental deterioration is progressive and they're dead. I hope that's the case, because if it isn't and they're still out there, they might someday be able to duplicate Laurie Carter's discovery. And if they do, their name will be legion.

Part 4: TRANSMISSION ERRORS

Terry Ryan was still sulking a week after the move, even though she admitted to herself that her new bedroom was a lot better than the tiny one she'd had when they'd lived in the apartment in Providence. Her parents had decided that reasoning with her would only prolong what they saw as a manufactured crisis. "We're not even that far away. You can take a bus into the city and see your friends on weekends." But Terry insisted that it wasn't the same. "I'll always just be a visitor. I won't be part of things anymore." Sixteen is a very difficult age.

She was also determined to have nothing to do with the inhabitants of Managansett, adult or otherwise. It was fairly easy to avoid kids her own age since it was summer and school was out. There wasn't much to do in a small town that didn't have a mall, a movie theater, or even a fast food restaurant. For any of those things she would have had to walk or bus out to the shopping center just east of town on Route 13. But rather than make even a rudimentary effort, she left the house after breakfast each morning and explored the labyrinth of paths through the woods on the north side of town. Occasionally she encountered other people there but she never spoke to any of them. She had always enjoyed hiking in the woods, and in that at least Managansett was well provided.

Sometimes she went home to eat – her parents were both at work so she had to fend for herself – and they each took one of the cars, so she couldn't drive to Providence. She probably would not have done so even if it had been possible. In order to maintain her sense of martyrdom, she had cut off virtually all contact with her friends there. Occasionally she made sandwiches and packed them with a couple of cans of soda and picnicked by herself. Within a couple of weeks of their arrival, she knew the area well enough not to get lost despite the bewildering number of paths and had found a half dozen spots that were both comfortable and private.

Halfway through her third week, right at the end of June, she decided to go further afield. There were half a dozen abandoned farms on the north side of the reservoir, variously boarded up or falling down. They had driven through the area while her parents were deciding whether or not to buy their first house and the decrepit buildings were still the first image that came to mind when Terry thought about her new home town. It was a comfortably warm Monday and she had two sandwiches and a banana in her backpack. She decided to explore.

She spotted one of the barns first but the roof and one wall had collapsed and she wasn't tempted to go inside. A small silo just beyond was locked up tight and the farmhouse proper had boards nailed across the doors and windows. Although she peered through some of the gaps, the gloom inside concealed whatever might be there from view. She sat on the porch and ate one of her sandwiches, then started across an overgrown field. The silhouette of another barn loomed above a line of poplars.

This one was in much better condition. The walls and roof were intact and there was a shiny new padlock on the door. The adjacent house needed a fresh coat of paint and some other work, but it was also in reasonable condition. The windows and doors were all unencumbered and there was a large pile of warped wooden boards sitting to one side. As Terry approached the front of the house, she realized that they had been recently removed. There was no indication that anyone was around, but she had the sudden feeling that the house was no longer abandoned. She turned back toward the barn and noticed that a shiny new electric meter had been installed on one side.

As that thought occurred to her, she heard a vehicle approaching.

If Terry had been thinking clearly, she would have walked back to the narrow road and continued on her way. But her first thought was that she was trespassing and that if anyone saw her and it got back to her parents, she would be on the defensive, which would undermine her stance that she was being treated unfairly. So she turned and walked quickly away from the road, concealing herself behind a corner of the house.

She expected the vehicle – it sounded like a truck – to go on by but it slowed and turned into the dirt driveway. Terry's heart caught in her throat and she shrank back further, glancing around in search of an escape route. There were a few bushes nearby but there was too much open space between the house and the woods. Anyone looking in the right direction would be sure to spot her.

It was a rental truck, fairly large, and it drove past the front of the house and up to the barn door. A minivan followed and four men spilled out of it to join two from the truck. They began unloading immediately, lots of small boxes, several pieces of electronic equipment, and finally a large glass dome big enough that Terry could easily have stood upright inside. One of the men unlocked the padlocked doors and swung them open. He seemed to be in charge and Terry noticed him particularly because he was short and very slender, with a dark complexion. She thought he might be Indian or Pakistani or maybe even an Afghan. The men spoke among themselves but she was too far away to hear anything.

It took about an hour to move everything into the barn. Apparently it needed to be arranged because all six men disappeared from view and that's when Terry ran to the line of trees and made her way home.

It rained for the next two days and Terry was stuck in the house, which she told herself she hated passionately, even though she had to admit that it was attractively laid out, with more room than the three of them actually needed. There were five bedrooms and her father had told her she could take the small one adjacent to her bedroom as a study room or whatever. She had responded without enthusiasm but the prospect secretly pleased her, although she had no idea yet what she would do with so much empty space.

Thursday morning was misty but the skies cleared rapidly. Terry packed herself another lunch – tuna fish this time – and left the house by nine.

Although she had not consciously decided to check out the activity at the farm, she found herself eating lunch not far away. When she was done, she started along the road. It appeared to be deserted again. She stood watching for quite a while, then took advantage of a line of unkempt bushes to circle around behind the barn. From this new vantage point, she saw a smaller, person sized door at the back, and it had a small, square window inset. There were no vehicles anywhere on the property, no sounds from house or barn, and she finally decided to take a chance. She could always say she was just sightseeing and thought the farm was abandoned.

Ordinarily she would have been unable to see much through the dirty window, but there were lights on inside, one at each end of the barn. They didn't help much, but she spotted the dome she'd seen on her previous visit placed flush against one wall. Except that when she squinted and looked closer, she saw that there were two of them, side by side. There was much more of the other equipment than she remembered as well, so obviously the truck had made more than one delivery.

She tried the door but it was locked.

Emboldened, she crossed to the house and made a complete circuit, peering in through the windows. There were no lights here but there were signs of recent activity. There were boxes in several of the ground floor rooms – some opened and some not – and there were stack of books, file folders, and other paperwork scattered around. In the large front room there were two modern modular work stations with computers, printers, and scanners. There were no personal effects that she could see and it looked more like an office than living space.

Her curiosity aroused, she decided to return regularly, but her plans were disrupted once again, this time without outside intervention. On her way home, she attempted to jump across a narrow brook and landed badly, twisting her ankle and wrenching her knee. It didn't seem broken but her entire leg ached like crazy and by the time she got home the ankle had swollen so badly that she had trouble taking off her sneaker, and she couldn't bend her knee without wincing. She soaked the ankle in cold water, which seemed to help, and put an icepack on her knee, but when she tried to put weight on that leg, she fell to the floor.

"That's a pretty bad strain you've got there," said Doctor Pippin. "You've also bruised some tendons in your knee." Terry found herself pretty much confined to bed for the next several days. Even when the pain went away and she could move without limping, her injured ankle complained if she demanded too much of it and her knee was stiff. It was another week before she felt well enough to resume her extended hikes. But it was the middle of July now and oppressively hot, so her first few outings were too brief for her to revisit the farm and satisfy her curiosity. She considered borrowing the car one evening and driving by, but refusing to ask for such favors was part of her campaign of martyrdom – although she was beginning to tire of it herself – and she refrained.

But her injuries continued to mend and toward the end of the month the weather moderated enough that she began extending her walks until she finally thought she could manage a round trip to the farm. And so she went.

At first she could see nothing new. The barn doors were closed and there were no vehicles around. The house looked as dreary as always. But when she came closer she discovered that something new had been added. A prefabricated metal shed of considerable size had been erected behind the barn. She could hear a faint humming from within and several thick cables snaked along the ground and disappeared through new holes in the barn walls. She was looking through the small window into a much more crowded interior than she remembered when she heard someone drive up the road and turn into the driveway.

Terry didn't quite panic but she beat a hasty retreat and crouched down behind the hut wherein, obviously, a powerful generator hummed to itself. By inching along to the opposite end and peering around one corner, she could see two men standing in the yard beside a red pickup truck. One of them was the slender man she had seen during her first visit. The second was much taller and heavier, with a shock of thick white hair and an equally impressive beard. This time she could hear what they were saying.

"The last of the equipment from the house has been delivered and we've duplicated the configuration as closely as we could. I say it's time to start experimenting." The man with the beard had a gravelly voice but there was a hint of weakness that undercut it.

"We have barely started to reconstruct Wrentham's notes," said the other. He had a faint but persistent accent. "The niece may not have kept everything together. We know that her partner had duplicated the process and was even further along than she was. If we'd been able to obtain her records, it would have saved us a great deal of time."

"That's a dead end. Her laboratory was completely destroyed in the fire and she and her husband both are both dead. If she left anything helpful behind, we have no way of finding it."

They parted then. The bearded man started for the barn and the other went toward the house. Terry pulled her head back lest she be seen and wondered if she dared cross the field behind the barn and disappear into the woodlot beyond. But the ghost of an idea entered her mind and even though she told herself it was unwise and irresponsible and not entirely honest, she found it increasingly appealing.

Both men were out of sight when she stepped out from behind the generator building. Her pulse had quickened and she still wasn't sure she was doing the right thing, but she slipped the water bottle out of the side of her backpack and poured what remained onto the ground. Then she walked quickly and directly to the front door of the house.

The doorbell was rusted and probably not working so she knocked. For a few seconds nothing happened and she felt a disloyal sense of relief, but then the door opened and the slender man was looking at her suspiciously.

"Hi! I'm really sorry to bother you but I was out hiking and I ran out of water and it's really hot. I was starting to get lightheaded. Could I please refill my water bottle? I'm really sorry if I'm intruding, but you're the only house in the area."

It all came out a bit too quickly but she figured that it would be natural for her to be nervous under the circumstances. The man didn't react at first, was clearly thinking about it, but then he nodded and stepped back. "Please come in."

The front room was pretty much as she remembered it except the piles of books seemed to be higher and more numerous. Both computers were on and she spotted a high end scanner/printer and what looked like external hard drives, although there were at least a dozen of them, which seemed unlikely. There was dust everywhere except around the work stations.

"The kitchen is through there." The man pointed at an archway and Terry smiled and moved in that direction

"Thanks so much. I didn't know anyone was living out here. Did you move in recently?"

"Yes, quite recently."

The kitchen was dingy and dirty, although some effort had been made to clean it. There were dishes and coffee cups in the sink but no pans on the stove. A shiny new microwave stood on one counter, beside a Keurig coffee machine. There was a large refrigerator, which did not seem to have been turned on, and a smaller, office sized one which clearly had been. A key box had been mounted on one wall. The door was open and she could see that at least four of the hooks were filled with keys. Terry went to the sink and filled her water bottle. The pipes groaned a bit before the water came.

She turned, capping the bottle. He was standing in the doorway, watching her expressionlessly. "Thanks again, Mr...?"

He stirred and frowned, apparently trying to decide whether or not to answer. "Dal. I am Dr. Dal."

They were interrupted at that point by someone shouting from the front of the house. "Ram! Where are you?"

Dr. Dal turned and returned to the front room. Terry followed, glanced at the key box and read the labels: Generator, Barn, House, Console. There were three keys on the one labeled "Barn" and she impulsively took one before following Dal. The bearded man was with him now and he gave her a decidedly unfriendly look.

"The young lady was just leaving," said Dal. His voice was pleasant but it was clearly an order.

"It was a pleasure meeting you, sir." She slipped past the other man, who remained silent, and left the house. When she got home, she hid the purloined key inside a stuffed bear.

It took her a while to find Dr. Ramiran Dal on the internet because she guessed "Dahl" and "Dall" and even "Doll" before a fuzzy search succeeded. There wasn't a lot of information. He was a physicist who, at least until recently, had been employed by Technosolve Industries, which worked primarily in the field of environmental reclamation. She had memorized the license plate on the truck and searched on that, but came up empty.

She didn't dare go back the following day because that might make the two men suspicious, but she made an effort to be pleasant to her parents at breakfast. Terry had begun to tire of her role as the silently suffering martyr and had recast herself as a master spy. She was determined to ferret out Dr. Dal's secrets, but summer was half over and she knew that if she hadn't succeeded by the time school opened, other demands upon her time would probably bring her investigation to an end.

That evening she asked if she could borrow a car. "I want to go over to the shopping center for a while."

Delighted at the thaw, her parents fell over one another giving permission and she was soon behind the wheel of her mother's Toyota. That part went well, but she discovered that finding the farm by car wasn't as easy as doing so walking along familiar footpaths. Particularly in the dark. She missed the turn the first time and made it all the way to the Loft, a nightclub on the edge of town, before realizing her mistake. Then she took the wrong fork when the road split and had to backtrack again. Finally she drove right past the farm – she couldn't see any lights from the road – before realizing where she was.

She found a place where she could pull off the road and walked back. Except for the usual night noises, it was completely silent. On foot, she did notice a dim security light over the front door of the barn but the house was completely dark and the truck was gone. During her brief visit, Terry had sensed that no one was actually living in the house and she saw nothing now to contradict her opinion. '

Although she had brought a flashlight, she used it infrequently and always kept it pointed at the ground so that it couldn't be seen from a distance. She explored the grounds thoroughly. The generator was still working and when she peered through the rear door into the barn, everything there was as she remembered it. All of the shades had been drawn on the house. Someone had finally removed the pile of wooden boards, but no effort had been made to cut back the shrubs and weeds that crowded around the foundation. Terry doused the light and walked to the front of the barn.

She stood there for a while, fingering the key in the pocket of her jeans. Although she was quite confident that no one was around, she worried that the barn was alarmed. If there had been, she thought there would have to be a telephone line if it was monitored and she couldn't find anything that looked like one. Her car was five minutes away, less if she ran, and she doubted that any of the town police would be in the immediate area. It seemed like a safe gamble.

She unlocked the padlock, removed it from the hasp, and eased the door slightly open. There were no flashing lights, no wailing sirens, or any other indication that her entrance had tripped anything, but she supposed there could be a silent alarm. She decided to limit her visit to five minutes and then leave as quickly as possible. It seemed an acceptable risk.

There were switches to her right but she was not tempted to touch them. The two security lights were good enough for a quick look around. What she found was rather disappointing. Most of it she had already seen through the window and what she hadn't was more of the same. She did notice that the two big tanks were labeled. One said "Scanning" and the other "Reassembly." That really didn't tell her anything. There was a smaller tank on the opposite side of the barn which was labeled "Processing" and which he hadn't been able to see clearly from the outside. Now she noticed that it was filled with multiple spiral blades, similar to those in her mother's blender except much larger. Ductwork from behind this tank curled up over her head and connected to "Reassembly".

There were boxes and bags of various substances piled up beside it. She recognized charcoal and two different kinds of fertilizer and chalk but most of the others bore chemical names unfamiliar to her. A good sized water tank stood behind them, with a hose connecting it to "Processing." Terry was puzzled, but she also realized that she had overstayed her allotted time. Reluctantly, she went back outside, secured the padlock, and walked back to the car. But she had a plan.

She had forgotten that it was Friday and that she had agreed to accompany her mother on a visit to relatives in Boston the following day. Then it rained furiously on Sunday. Terry fretted and sulked and her parents thought she was reverting to her former mood, but it cleared late in the day and the forecast for the rest of the week was clear, but hot and humid. She insisted on making chocolate chip cookies that evening but she'd spent so little time in the kitchen – had no patience for cooking – that her mother ended up doing most of the work.

The following morning Terry packed half of the cookies in a metal tin, made two sandwiches for herself, bundled them into her backpack, and started walking.

It seemed to take longer than usual, but that was probably because she was anxious to arrive, and in fact she was close to the farm by late morning. Terry was having doubts about her plan. If there was no one there when she arrived, this would all have been for nothing. But she figured that they worked there during the day – on whatever it was that they were doing – and went home to wherever that was each evening. It still wasn't clear to her just what she was investigating, but it couldn't be a government project. It was too small and amateurish. They might be terrorists, and Terry had visions of appearing on television as the heroic teenager who uncovered a plot against America. But most of the time she assumed it was nothing quite so dramatic.

There were two vehicles parked in front of the barn when she arrived. One was the familiar small truck, the other a late model Honda. She had brought a pen and notebook this time and she wrote down the new license number. The barn doors were partly open and the lights were on inside, but she couldn't see anyone around.

She crossed the road and started toward the barn, making no effort to conceal herself. There were unidentifiable sounds coming from beyond the doors, a kind of sloshing like the washing machine made, and a constant buzzing that must have been electrical. She had nearly reached the doors when she heard voices.

"I told you. All of the equipment is working just as it was designed. I hardly needed to replace anything." It was the beaded man's voice.

Terry hesitated beside the Honda, glanced in through the passenger side window. There were some envelopes on the seat addressed to Howard Davenport at an address in Cranston. She jotted the information down in her notebook and put it back in her pocket.

Dr. Dal's voice responded after a lengthy pause. "I was always confident that the hardware was functional, Howard. It's the software that is suspect. I recovered more than twenty variations of the control program for the scanner. They were clearly having trouble with that side of the process as well as with the reassembler."

"Well, isn't it logical that the most recent version is the one we want?"

"You forget that the output was seriously flawed when we tried it. No, none of the existing programs are satisfactory, and I must understand the process that Wrentham and his niece and her associate employed if I am to correct their errors."

Their voices were growing louder and Terry realized they were coming outside. She had to act now or give away the fact that she'd been eavesdropping. She stepped forward to meet them, smiling broadly.

Neither of them smiled back. Dr. Dal looked momentarily stunned, then impassive. Davenport, as she assumed the other man must be, was clearly hostile.

"Hello again!" she said cheerfully. "I just wanted to stop by to thank you for the other day." She proffered the tin of cookies. "I baked these last night and wanted to drop them off."

The two men exchanged cryptic looks. "This was not necessary," said Dal at last. He accepted the tin awkwardly, looking as though he had no idea what it might be but suspected it was a bomb of some sort.

"It's nothing. I always make too many and they'll just go to waste."

Davenport made an impatient noise and Dal spoke up again. "We're actually quite busy at the moment."

"Oh, I don't want to bother you. I'm just passing by." She pulled out her recently emptied water bottle. "But would you mind another fill up? It's really hot again today."

Dal hesitated but nodded. "Come with me." She turned to follow him, but not before noticing that Davenport was scowling at her.

As soon as they were inside, Terry made immediately for the kitchen. "I'll be out of your hair in just a second." She refilled her bottle quickly. Dal hadn't followed her but had bent down to examine something on one of the computer screens. It was the moment Terry had been waiting for. She hastily replaced the purloined key on its hook – she had had a duplicate made at the local hardware store – and then headed for the front door. "Thanks a lot. Bye."

Her heart was racing but she managed to walk at a leisurely pace past the barn and down to the road. Davenport was nowhere in sight and the doors were closed.

Davenport was a very common name and it took her a long time to separate him from the others on the internet, but she finally found a couple of fleeting references. The only item of significance was that he too had worked for TechnoSolve but had recently resigned. So maybe they were working on some clandestine project for their new employer. But why out here in the sticks rather than in a modern laboratory?

Terry waited impatiently before going back. She didn't plan to be seen so she wore clothing that she thought would best blend in with the brush and foliage that pockmarked the property. It was a Sunday and she thought this would be the most likely day for the farm to be abandoned. She packed yet another light lunch, told her parents once more that she wanted to walk in the woods rather than drive to the mall. They were clearly puzzled but she had been so much more pleasant the last couple of weeks that they were hesitant to say or do anything that might change her mood. As she was leaving, she impulsively picked up a small flashlight and slipped it into her pocket. She was still hesitant about turning on the lights in the barn.

It had cooled off a bit but she still worked up a sweat before reaching the road. She guessed it was pretty close to five miles to the farm but the paths meandered and the ground was broken for much of the way so it took a full two hours before she broke out into the open. Another fifteen minute and she could see her destination.

The duplicate key opened the padlock after some slight resistance. Terry planned to make a more thorough search of the interior this time, but she didn't want to leave the doors open. They would be clearly visible from the street and for all she knew Dal and Davenport had the police watching the area when they were not around. She walked the length of the barn quickly, barely glancing around, and exited through the small rear door, propping it open with her backpack. She returned to the front, closed the big doors, and forced the padlock shut, then went back to the rear, retrieved her pack, and went inside.

It took a few seconds for her eyes to adjust to the dim light. As far as she could tell, nothing had changed since her last clandestine visit. She had time now to take in more details, like a thick panel of electronics suspended behind the two big tanks, one end connected to each, and a computer workstation tucked around to one side of "Scanning" and attached to it by a half dozen cables. She found that both domes had latching glass door and she opened each and peered inside, but both seemed to be completely empty.

She looked over the workstation briefly but was afraid to power it on and she guessed it would be password protected in any case. There was some paperwork on a shelf and she looked through it, but part of it was mathematics, part computer coding, and part diagrams of some kind of lab set up that she didn't recognize. Science had never been one of her better subjects. The "Processing" tank had a filmy residue at the bottom. There was no door to this one but a large portion of the top lifted away when she pushed on it. The smell was strong and rancid, like garbage that had been left around for too long. She closed it hastily.

Terry was contemplating leaving when the decision was taken from her. She heard a vehicle close at hand. Someone had driven up to the barn. She started to run for the back door and almost immediately tripped over a cable, banging her still mildly tender left knee against the base of "Scanning" as she fell headlong. Panicking, she tried to get up but the knee protested painfully. There were muffled voices and then a click as the padlock was disengaged. On hands and knees, Terry scuttled behind a stack of cardboard boxes that apparently had been thrown into a corner. She pulled her arms and legs in as tightly as possible and kept her head down.

"And I'm saying again that we're being too cautious." That was unmistakably Davenport.

'I understand your frustration, Howard, but science is not so clear cut as your engineering. You always have a clear goal in mind and one or more obvious routes to get there. Science is necessarily more exploratory. Even the goal may change as we move forward."

"Not for me. The goal is to use Wrentham's discovery to get rich."

"And we will. But our tests to date have had unsatisfactory results. The duplicates display imperfections, sometime subtle, sometime obvious. I agree with you that much of this results from errors during reassembly, and our predecessors were of much the same mind. It may prove to be impossible to eliminate them entirely but as we refine the process, they should become less of a problem. The jewelry passed inspection, did it not?"

Davenport did not sound mollified. "Sure, but how many Victorian trinkets can we sell before someone starts asking where it all came from? Now if we could duplicate gold bars..."

Dal sighed audibly. "Actually we can, but we would have to first acquire an equivalent amount of gold in some other form. This is transformation we are dealing with, not transmutation."

"I know. I know. But the machine is operating, even if not optimally. We ought to be able to make that work for us."

"We haven't done badly. Over a hundred thousand dollars already, enough to keep us going."

"Chicken feed."

More lights came on suddenly and Terry tried to become even smaller. There was a rising hum and still more lights flickered. The two large domes were suddenly brightly illuminated.

"I believe it is possible that I...we have been looking at the wrong end of the problem. The reassembling process is of vital importance, of course, but it occurred to me this morning that perhaps a larger problem is inaccuracies during scanning. If the template is imperfect, the copies will necessarily replicate and magnify those discrepancies."

"Have you figured out how to interpret the scanning arrays?"

"I can correlate certain portions of the array to specific attributes, but no, I cannot say that I understand them except in the most imprecise way."

"So how will you know what's wrong?"

"I plan to make multiple scans of the same source. If the scanning is correct, there will be no discernible difference from one array to the next. If there are significant variations, then we need to determine the cause."

"Alright. Here, put my car keys in there and I'll initiate the sequence. How many copies do you want?"

"None right now. Just the scans. Copies will introduce the uncertainties in reassembly. I will compare the scans directly to one another in order to find variations, if any. But we need something more complex than a set of keys."

Terry peered around one corner of a box and saw the two men standing in front of the scanner. The glass door was open. Davenport was looking exasperated. "All right. Take a scan of me, unless you'd rather do the honors." He climbed into the chamber, which was tall enough for him to stand upright. Dal went to the console and the background hum changed pitch. There was a faint flash or strobe of light, but nothing seemed to have changed.

"Scan two initiated," said Dal and a second later the lights blinked again. There was a longer pause before he announced a third scan. As soon as the lights returned to normal, Davenport exited the chamber.

"Got what you needed?"

"Yes, but to be safe, I want a second data set. Will you do the honors?" Dal moved toward the scanning chamber, apparently intending to clamber inside, but at that very moment Terry leaned forward, lost her balance, and instinctively reached out to grab something stable. The pile of boxes went crashing down.

Terry rose and bolted for the back door and might even have made it because the two men were momentarily frozen. But her banged knee protested, she stumbled and almost fell, and before she could recover Davenport had hold of her arm. Her grip was tight and it hurt.

"What do you know? It's the cookie girl. I told you something wasn't right about her."

Dal looked unhappy. "What are you doing here, young lady? This is private property."

"And more to the point, how did you get in here?" Davenport glanced toward the rear of the barn. "You didn't leave the back door unlocked, did you, Dal?"

"I haven't used it since we moved the equipment in. Maybe she picked the lock."

"Let me go!" Terry tugged on her arm. "I wasn't doing anything."

"No," said Davenport. "But you probably got an earful." He turned to Dal. "We can't let her go. She might tell someone."

"What could she tell them? And we're doing nothing illegal in any case."

"She was spying on us. Who knows who she's working for. We might not be the only ones trying to track down Wrentham's discovery." He pulled her over to the scanning tank, glaring down at her.

"She's just a child, Howard."

Davenport looked thoughtful. With his free hand he opened the door to the scanning chamber, forced her inside before she could mount any real resistance, then closed the door, holding it shut with one hand. Terry was suddenly terrified.

"There's your second subject. Take your scans."

Dal looked doubtful, but he moved to the console and a few seconds later the lights blinked. "Let me out of here!" Terry shouted. She had felt nothing but she was still terrified. They blinked a second time and then a third.

The door opened and Terry almost leaped out. Davenport grabbed her arm again before she could bolt. "Let's all go into the house and talk this over."

"Just a minute," said Dal. "Let me disengage the storage module. I want to let the compiler run overnight so I can start working with this data first thing in the morning.

"We'll go ahead."

Neither of them said a word as Davenport half led, half dragged Terry to the house. He used a key to open the door and pushed her inside. Her knee was feeling better now and she thought she could run on it if she had the chance. But he was careful, not only staying between himself and the door but remaining close to her so that even when he relinquished his grip, she was within easy reach.

"I didn't mean anything. I'm sorry. I was just curious." Terry sensed that defiance would not work with this man, so she shifted to deference. "I won't do it again." But she still had the key in the pocket of her jeans.

"Give me your cell phone," he said.

"I don't have one." It was in her pocket. Her parents insisted that she carry it whenever she was off on her own.

'Don't give me that. All you kids have them. Hand it over or I'll take it."

Terry considered resisting but knew she had no choice. She gave it to him without another word.

He was quiet for an awkwardly long time and she didn't like the way he was looking at her. "All right," he said at last. "I suppose it won't do any harm if you see what we're keeping downstairs." He gestured for her to go into the kitchen. There was a little mudroom leading to the side yard. At the opposite end was a narrow door that she hadn't noticed before. "Open it and look if you want to."

Her curiosity took over. She pulled the door open and stared down into the darkness. There wasn't much light and she couldn't see anything and then he shoved her from behind and she was falling. Mercifully it wasn't a long drop and the floor was earthen and just knocked the wind out of her. But she banged her knee again on the lowest of a steep set of wooden steps and that hurt a lot more.

The door slammed behind her and she was in near total darkness.

Enough light crept in around the corners of the door that she had a general idea of her surroundings. At the top of the steprs she tried to open the door but it was latched shut and would not budge. She descended again and was feeling around with her hands when she remembered the small flashlight in her pocket. Exploring was much easier after that, but it was no more heartening. There were no windows and no other doors and except for some elderly glass jars on some rickety shelves at the back end, the room was empty. Terry found a relatively comfortable position to sit, turned off her flashlight, and started to think.

She could hear them talking upstairs. Arguing actually, and occasionally shouting. She caught enough of the conversation to understand that Dr. Dal wanted to let her go but that Davenport was resisting. Unfortunately he was the dominant half of the pair. The voices died down after an hour and then the door opened. Dal descended carrying a plate of sandwiches and some blankets.

"I am very sorry about this, young lady, but I am afraid you will have to stay here for a while. My friend is very angry with you and he is not reacting entirely rationally. I am sure that he will realize his error once he has had some time to reflect upon it. I have never known him to act this way until now. In the meantime, I hope these things will help."

Terry stood up, wondering if she could slip past him and run up the stairs, but a shadow moved in the doorway and she realized Davenport was standing there. "Thank you," she said insincerely.

He made a second trip down carry a pitcher of water and a bucket. Terry looked at the latter. "What's that for?" Then she realized its purpose and grimaced. He went back upstairs and the door closed. She heard a bolt slide home this time. Terry ate one of the sandwiches and then adjusted the blankets as best she could. At least it was relatively cool in the basement. After a while she fell asleep.

It was completely dark when she woke. She was cramped and chilly but she climbed the steps and tried the door. "Is anyone there?" There was no answer. She tried the door again, put more effort into it, and managed to shake it on its hinges, but there was no sign that she was accomplishing anything. After awhile, she went back to the blankets and slept again.

Davenport brought her a microwaved dinner – fish and cardboard veggies – at about midmorning. She had nothing to say to him and he left without speaking. An hour or so later she heard footsteps and Dr. Dal spoke through the door, asking if she was all right. She told him she wanted to go home.

"Yes, I understand that. I am making progress with my friend. Please be patient." And then he went away.

Davenport brought her dinner – it was a repeat of her lunch – and continued the silent treatment. Terry alternated between being frightened and being furious, but also lethargic. She dozed on and off throughout the day. Darkness fell and anger became her dominant emotion. They had no right to keep her locked up like this.

She was half asleep when she heard someone moving around upstairs. She stood up and walked to the stairs just as the lock slid back and the door opened. Suddenly wary, she backed away, wishing she had something to use as a weapon. A figure descended the steps halfway and flicked on a flashlight. Terry raised an arm to shield her eyes, but relaxed slightly. It was Dal.

"I am taking you home, child. I should have done this yesterday. I apologize for my weakness."

"It's about time," she snapped. "You people are in a lot of trouble, you know."

She had just started toward the stairs when there was a muffled shout and Dal seemed to fly toward her. He hit the ground hard enough to take his breath away. Terry didn't understand what had happened at first, but then she heard Davenport's voice.

"I thought I'd catch you out here. Equal partners my ass. You were going to let her go and ruin everything for both of us without even telling me. Well, Howard Davenport isn't the kind of man you mess with." And then he retreated back up the stairs, the door closed, and the bolt slid back into place.

Terry was still standing there, blinking, when Dal rolled over. "Well, I seem to have misjudged the situation." His voice was calm, resigned.

Terry thought about it. "You aren't getting any of my blankets." She went over and curled up on her makeshift bed to prove her point.

Neither of them knew what to expect in the morning and in fact the upstairs remained silent until well after the sun came up. Then they heard footsteps, at least two men. Terry was going to call out but Dr. Dal gestured for her to remain silent. "Let us listen for a while first."

After perhaps twenty minutes, the door opened and Davenport descended carrying two microwave meals – pasta this time but Terry was so hungry that she didn't really care. There was something odd about their captor. He seemed more diffident and less aggressive. Terry started to argue with him, insisting that she wouldn't say anything if he would just let her go. But then someone shouted down from the top of the stairs, and it was Davenport's voice, and a second figure loomed above them.

"Save your breath. Number Four may not be the brightest light on the tree but he'll do what I tell him."

Terry glanced back and forth between the two men, who were obviously twins. Their numerical advantage, whatever it might have been worth, was obviously gone. They accepted the meals and the two men vanished back upstairs.

"What was wrong with his brother?" she asked after a while. "Is he retarded or something?"

Dal had barely touched his food. He shook his head. "They're not brothers."

"But they look exactly alike. They were even dressed the same way."

"That's because they are the same person. After a fashion, anyway."

It took him a while to get started but once the words started to flow it was like a faucet that could no longer be shut off. He explained that he and Davenport had worked at Technosolve with a man named Carl Wrentham. "It was a desalinization project. You know, removing salt from sea water so that it is potable. Carl had his own ideas and we were working somewhat independently right from the start, but then he became very secretive after a while and that made Howard suspicious. He mentioned it to me and I became curious as well. We rather unethically visited Carl's laboratory one evening. Carl was already encrypting his notes and I believe he was taking the hard drive from one of his computers home with him at night, but we found enough to realize he had stumbled onto something revolutionary. Matter reassembly."

Terry wasn't all that interested but she was bored. "What's that?"

Dal took a deep breath. "You know that everything is made up of certain basic elements, right?"

"I took chemistry." But she'd barely managed a C.

"Well, matter cannot be created or destroyed and you can't make gold out of carbon or silver out of lead. But Carl discovered a method by which he could shift things around. We can take a lump of gold and reassemble it into a broach or a necklace, so long as we have a schematic of the item we want. So we conduct a kind of scan of an object – although it is more than that; it's a complete mapping of every atom in that object. Then, assuming we have all of the raw materials that are required, we can reshape them into an exact duplicate." He paused. "Theoretically. We haven't completely mastered the reassembly process. Carl was probably working on that when he died."

Terry thought about it. She was intelligent and quick witted enough to see some of the implications. "So you could take a pile of paper and the right ink and copy a stack of money?"

"In theory, yes. But there would be small flaws. Most would be invisible without a microscope but some would not. We would not want to be caught passing counterfeit money. But there are other items where this would not be so much of a problem."

"Sounds cool, but why all the secrecy?"

Dal sighed. "We are not ready for the public to know about the process, and the methods by which we acquired some of the documentation and equipment were not completely lawful. There is also the possibility that legal action would be taken to prevent us from duplicating objects where are protected by copyright, patent, or other means. Please realize that in the long term our intentions are, or at least were, aboveboard and honorable, but we decided to employ great discretion at this stage. Howard purchased this property from his savings and we have both resigned from our jobs to devote ourselves to the project. We have had to resort to using the equipment, faulty though it may be, to finance our efforts."

"So what does all of this have to do with the brothers?"

Dal sighed again, louder this time. "It is possible to reassemble organics as well as inorganics."

"What does that mean?"

"Howard scanned himself the night we found you in the barn. He has obviously made a duplicate of himself to help him. The duplicate is imperfect, as expected."

"You mean he copied himself?"

"Yes, essentially. But I am also concerned by something else he said. He referred to his...copy as Number Four. That suggests that there is a Number Two and Three, and possibly even a One if he does not include himself."

"There are five of him now?" Terry shook her head. This was not something she could wrap her head around.

"I believe so, unless some of the others were non-viable. We know from Carl's notes that when he duplicated living beings, they often died quickly or were deficient in other ways."

"But what would he do with all the bodies? Bury them?"

"No, that would be wasteful. He would cut them up and put them in the processor to be stored until their constituent elements were needed."

Terry fell silent after that, but Dal could not stop now that he had started. "Not only do the copies have defects, but later copies from the initial scan seem to indicate that the deterioration is progressive. Carl's niece and a friend of hers tried to refine the process – they are also both dead now – by rescanning the original object each time. To their surprise and my own, copies made from newer scans continued rather than paralleled the drop in quality of the copies. They concluded that at least part of the problem was in the scanning process itself. I believe that they were correct. I have found subtle variations in scans taken within a few seconds of each other, subtle but much greater than simply because of normal ongoing biological processes."

Terry was still struggling with the vision of body parts being dropped into the giant blender she'd seen in the barn, so she wasn't really paying attention. "None of that is going to get us out of here and that's all I care about right now."

And this finally stemmed the flow of words, at least for the moment.

Number Four brought them pasta for lunch again. He didn't say anything but he only came down a few steps before setting down the two platters. It tasted exactly the same but Dr. Dal regarded it suspiciously. "Howard scanned all the groceries so we wouldn't have to go shopping again. He just assembles a new copy when it's time to eat."

Terry thought about that. "Can this stuff poison us?"

He shook his head. "Not now. But the copies will continue to vary from the original. They may start tasting wrong and looking slightly different."

"Hard to tell what it looks like down here."

"I have a concern." He set aside his foot almost untouched. "There is a possibility that I had not considered before. I have known Howard for a long time and his behavior the past two days has not been consistent with his personality. He is more aggressive, less rational, and has become impulsive. I have never known him to act precipitately or without considerable forethought."

Terry wasn't quite as enthusiastic about the food as she had been, but she was hungry and began eating again.

"We always assumed that the scanning process was non-invasive. I must now entertain the possibility that this was an unjustified supposition and that the recording process is interactive. That would explain why rescanning the original does not solve the problem of deterioration."

"I have no idea what you're talking about. And if you're not going to eat that, hand it over."

Dal passed over his platter. "Howard has been scanned three times. Each of those scans may have introduced anomalies into his body. One of the most vulnerable organs is the brain. It is possible that the process has altered his personality. The copies will be even more degraded, as is the case with our jailer."

Terry considered what he'd said. "You scanned me three times."

He nodded. "I have no standard by which to evaluate whether or not your personality has changed."

She shrugged. "I feel perfectly normal."

"The changes would vary from individual to individual. It may be that in your case the alterations were much smaller or that they were not in the area of personality. There is no reason for you to become alarmed."

Actually, she wasn't particularly worried. But she did feel a growing sense of outrage. "You had no right to do that to me."

"I believed it could do you no harm, and I may be wrong about the scanner. Howard might have had some kind of breakdown."

"You said this Wrentham guy died?"

He nodded. "Yes. He was found dead outside his home. An autopsy was unable to find a cause of death. But there is no evidence that he ever scanned himself."

"What about the others? Didn't you say some more of them died?"

"His niece disappeared. Her body was never found. She was working with another woman who later died in an accident at her home. There is no reason to believe that either death was connected to their experiments."

That afternoon they discussed an escape plan. Terry didn't particularly like it but she had nothing better to suggest. Then they sat and waited for their dinner to arrive. It seemed to take forever before they heard the door open.

Dal mounted the stairs to accept the two trays and then made as if to descend, but immediately stopped and raised his voice. "This isn't even hot. Do you expect us to eat this?"

Number Four was about to close the door and he hesitated. The next few seconds were vital to their plan. Dal climbed higher, holding out the food in front of him. "This needs more time in the microwave. You have to take it back."

There was a rumble in the bigger man's throat, but he seemed incapable of speech. Perhaps he was. "Take it, I tell you!" Dal thrust them forward more forcefully. Number Four started to reach for them, hesitated. "All right. Take me to the kitchen and I'll do it myself. You can stay with me so that I can't run off." And he went up another step.

Terry was crouched at the bottom, waiting for her moment. Dal had to make it through the door if she was to have any chance. By sheer bluff he continued forward and Number Four took a hesitant step back. Terry started up the steps, moving as quietly as possible. Dal had moved out of her line of sight, but Number Four reacted at last. He stepped across the doorway and reached out for the slender man, who nimbly evaded his grasp, still ostensibly headed for the kitchen. She couldn't wait any longer. She ran up the last few steps and lunged past him. She almost made it but he reached out at the last possible second and caught a handful of her long hair. Terry cried out as he jerked her head back, then turned to kick him.

Number Four took the blow on his hip and relinquished his grip. Terry pulled back and lost her balance, falling heavily to the floor. He towered over her and she began to scramble back into the space between an overstuffed Victorian sofa and the wall. As she did so, she saw Dal emerge from the kitchen, holding a large knife above his head. He plunged it into Number Four's back. She saw the face register surprise, then confusion, then nothing at all as he fell forward, his dead weight pinning her to the floor.

There was a crash and shouting and she realized that Howard Davenport – or at least another one of him – had entered the fray. The dead one was so heavy that it took her a few seconds to slide out from beneath him and then get shakily to her feet. At the entranceway to the kitchen, a Davenport had caught hold of Dr. Dal and was choking him. Terry knew she should run to the door and off into the woods, bring help. But the help would be too late for Dr. Dal. And she found that she hated Howard Davenport with an intensity that was almost frightening.

The knife in Number Four's back wouldn't come out at first, but she put a foot on the dead man's buttocks and heaved it free. She raised it above her head with both hands and approached the struggling twosome, although Dal no longer seemed to be struggling. Then she brought it down as hard as she could in the center of Davenport's back, just below the neck.

At first he hardly seemed to notice. But then his hands opened and Dal's limp form fell to the floor. Davenport turned around and regarded her balefully, one hand reaching back to try to reach the hilt of the knife. But then his eyes glazed and he took a single step forward before falling headlong.

Terry waited until she was sure he wasn't moving, then went to check on Dal. He was dead as well.

She sat on the floor beside him for a while, then stood up and began emptying the boxes of paper all around the room, kicked over the stacks of book until they were distributed fairly evenly. At first she thought she might have to find a way to start an electrical fire somehow, but then she found a packet of matches in the kitchen and that made it a lot easier. When she left the house, the front room was already ablaze.

The barn was open but she entered cautiously. She remembered that there might well be at least two more Howard Davenports at large. But then she saw what was in the three plastic tubs arranged around the processor and realized that for whatever reason, the original had decided to dispense with Number Two and Number Three. There were at least three arms waiting to be reprocessed.

It was a little more difficult to start a fire there, but she managed, and once it was going she carried flaming bits of paper or wood into all four corners so that the entire building would be consumed. Satisfied at last, she started the long walk home.

The story made the national news. Terry had rehearsed her version of events during the hike back to the house. She told her parents, and the police, and the reporters that she had been out hiking when the two men had forced her into a pickup trip and imprisoned her in the basement of a farmhouse. "I think there was a third man, but I never saw him, just heard them talking upstairs."

No, she hadn't been sexually assaulted and no, she didn't know what they had wanted from her. They had started arguing among themselves almost immediately. When the fire started, she had thought she was trapped, but one of them had opened the door and told her to get out while she could. She was pretty sure that he was hurt in some way but she hadn't stayed around to find out. The barn was already burning when she got outside and no, she had no idea why they had torched either or both buildings. She had just run while she could, hiding in the woods until she knew they weren't looking for her, and then made her way home.

For a while, she checked herself in the mirror a lot and tried to decide if she had changed in any way, but she decided she was worried about nothing. She felt pretty good overall, more alive than ever before.

The spotlight moved quickly away from her thanks to a school shooting in Taunton and a terrorist attack in Zurich. By the end of August, her life was almost back to normal.

But then Terry told her parents that she had decided to drop out of school and the argument raged for hours until she went out to the kitchen, picked out a knife, and then stabbed her mother in the living room and her father out in the garage. She couldn't understand why she hadn't killed them months earlier.

Part 5: BACK UP COPIES

.Chloe Wrentham had not been declared legally dead because no trace of her body was ever found her partner insisted that she had no idea where her friend had gone or what had happened to her. The court appointed administrator arranged for the house to be closed up, the pipes drained, utilities discontinued, mail forwarded to his office where a clerk would deal with it, and promptly forgot about the property. The presumed deceased had no known living relatives, so no one objected.

And one day three panel trucks drove up and a team of men opened the house and removed a great deal of equipment including computers, glass walled chambers, and sophisticated if unorthodox electronics. The neighbors were mildly curious, but no one asked what was going on and eventually the trucks drove away.

The Van Horn family had owned Highpoint Lodge for as long as Damon Sanders had lived in Boynton and he'd been there for nearly three decades. It had always seemed wasteful to him because the family never occupied it more than once a year, if then, and never for longer than a couple of weeks. There was a maintenance staff year round, of course, because the Lodge was an expensive piece of property, but they were frequently replaced and none of them had ever really become a part of the community.

That had all changed a few months earlier. The first hint of an alteration was when three large trucks and a limousine had passed through town one morning, turning on the private road that led up a winding path to the crest where the Lodge was set overlooking an adjacent valley. Within a few days several more vehicles had followed the same route, and it was obvious that the Lodge was going to be occupied even though winter had yet to relax its grip and the scenic views were still slumbering under coarse blankets of snow and pine needles. Even more puzzling was the arrival of four vehicles marked "Abrams Security Services." In the past, Arthur Van Horn had relied upon his personal staff and the local police to protect his property and his privacy.

Charlie White was the first local to see some of what was going on. He was an electrician and he'd been hired to help with some "renovations." The first night he showed up at the Black Goat Tavern shaking his head. "You should see the mess they've made up to the Lodge. Tore out a bunch of walls to make one big room at the back. It'll take a week to lay all the wiring they want."

"Maybe they're going to turn it into a restaurant or something," suggested Norm Palmer nervously. Norm owned the only restaurant in Boynton that wasn't a fast food place or a diner.

"They've got a lot of equipment up there waiting to be installed," said Charlie, "but it's nothing I recognize. Some kind of laboratory maybe."

Bits and pieces of information emerged intermittently during the next few days. Van Horn acknowledged Mayor Soames' welcome tersely but didn't invite him to come inside for his customary glass of brandy. This wasn't entirely surprising as everyone knew that Adele Van Horn was the only reason there had been any social intercourse between Lodge and town in the past and she had died the previous fall in an automobile accident. Their only child, a boy in his late teens, had been seriously injured at the same time and Charlie White had seen him sitting in a wheelchair while he was laying wire. "I said hello once but he just kept staring off into space."

Some people were miffed when the security fence went up. It was not uncommon for the local people to hike up to the crest beyond the Lodge to enjoy the view. It was still possible because part of the crest was public land, but detouring around the fence added as much as an hour to the round trip. Chief Granger just shrugged. "It's his property and his business what he does with it, but there's never been a report of a crime up near the Lodge in thirty years."

There was an undercurrent of resentment that persisted but it was ameliorated somewhat when the Lodge began ordering groceries and other supplies locally, pumping some fresh cash into the moribund economy. Some of the greatly augmented staff drove down occasionally to eat at Palmer's restaurant or shop in the small commercial district, although no one patronized the Boynton Theater. The Lodge had an impressive private theater of its own.

Most astonishing of all, it appeared that the Van Horns were planning a prolonged stay. One of the guards told a bartender that they had a six month contract and word spread through the town.

Those who were likely to profit by the influx of new customers were happy to hear the news, but there were others who wondered just what it was that had brought about this change of affairs. Rumors that the boy, Peter, was brain damaged seemed to be the most likely explanation. And in a sense, that was true.

Damon Sanders was one of those few who didn't care either way. He had moved to Boynton because he wanted a quiet place where he could write his detective stories and avoid his fans. If the shops were a little more crowded than before, it didn't matter greatly because Damon didn't visit them often. He lived a rather simple, routine life, working at his computer four hours a day, cooking most of his own meals, keeping his small cottage clean and orderly, and taking long walks through the almost untouched forests that surrounded Boynton on every side. He knew that the interstate loomed off to the east, that there was a small city directly south, several farms a few miles westward, and a shopping mall not far to the north, but he never walked far enough for any of these to impose upon his enjoyment of the world.

Damon might not always be happy but he was invariably content. If only things had stayed that way.

If he hadn't twisted his ankle, he might never have ventured inside the Lodge. If he hadn't been friendly with one of the security guards, he might never have twisted his ankle. But life is filled with things we might have done but didn't, and choices we might have made differently.

Damon's walks followed a few regular itineraries but he was particularly fond of the view from the crest and he often packed a sandwich and some bottled water and headed that way after finishing his daily quota of words. The security fence had caused him to swerve slightly from the most popular path but his home was sufficiently far from the town proper that it added only a few minutes to his journey and he had no feelings of resentment. There was a short stretch over very broken grown just where the fence changed directions and he was passing there early one afternoon when he spotted a uniformed guard balancing awkwardly atop a small rocky outcrop as he tried to reach a security camera nestled in the crook of a branch above his head.

Their eyes met and Damon waved. The guard tried to wave back, lost his balance, and fell heavily into some brush.

Damon rushed over as quickly as he could manage over the broken ground, but the fence interposed itself. He knew there was a gate at the top of the next rise but he had never seen it unlocked. "Are you all right?" he called through the fence, unable to see the guard.

A few seconds passed before someone swore heavily and there was a stirring in the brush. "Yeah, I'm fine. Just had the breath knocked out of me." The guard sat up. He was in his late twenties as best Damon could judge, clean shaven, crew cut, with sturdy and not unhandsome features.

"What were you trying to do anyway?"

"The camera's angled the wrong way. It was working all right until last night. The night guy says he thinks a bat flew into it."

Damon glanced up at the camera. It seemed to be directed at a point well over his head. "This place looks more like a prison than a vacation home."

The guard was standing now, brushing off his pants. They were black, as was his jacket and tie, the former emblazoned with the name Abrams. "The old man likes his security, all right. If he's willing to pay us to watch squirrels and birds, it's fine with me. I'm Jim, by the way." He extended his hand as though to shake, but the mesh of the fence prevented that. Damon gave a little wave of acknowledgement and identified himself.

"You wouldn't happen to have a spare one of those?" asked the guard. He gestured toward his mouth to indicate the cigarette Damon was smoking.

"Oh, sure." He passed one through the fence, along with his lighter.

Jim lit up, took a long draw, and passed back the lighter. "Thanks. We're not allowed to smoke back at the Lodge because of the kid. He has breathing problems."

"Van Horn's son?"

"Yeah. Rough situation there. Almost completely paralyzed from the waist down. Sometimes they have to put him under an oxygen tent because his lungs stop working. I'd rather be dead myself."

They parted amicably and a few days later when Damon ventured along the same path, he spotted Jim up ahead, walking along the fence line, and took a short detour to say hello. Jim was assigned to patrol a quarter mile of perimeter fence, six days a week. "Boring as hell." They talked for another few minutes and that set the pattern. Once or occasionally twice a week they'd meet, sometimes have a smoke together, and then move on along their predetermined courses. They weren't really friends, but neither were they strangers. Jim had no idea why so much security was required and Damon didn't really care enough to wonder about it.

Toward the end of May, Damon took a tumble. He was near Jim' stretch of perimeter but hadn't seen anyone about. He had chosen this path because he always felt constrained to help break the monotony of Jim's job however briefly, but since he wasn't really in the mood for conversation that day, he turned away and quickened his pace, obligation satisfied. There was a wide, steep, and uneven ridge of rock and loose sand which he had to cross and just short of the top a stone turned under his right foot. He overcompensated, staggered, his left foot was caught between two stones and he fell awkwardly backward, stunning himself.

He lay there for a minute or two before recognizing that the pain in his left ankle was intense. An attempt to move his leg failed and he felt a flash of panic, forced himself to calm down, then maneuvered his foot slowly until he was finally able to lift it free. He was convinced that he had broken his ankle – it was actually just very badly sprained – and knew that he would never make it back down to the road, let alone home, without assistance.

Slowly, painfully, he swiveled his body around so that he could look down toward the security fence. His satisfaction that Jim had not been present quickly turned to irritation that he wasn't around when needed. It was about fifteen minutes later – although it seemed like more than an hour – when the tall, dark garbed guard came into view, picking his way through the brush.

Damon called out, explained his situation, and Jim took the radio from his belt.

A team of four people came for him. Jim unlocked the gate and they carried out a stretcher and first aid kit. All four were young and earnest looking. Three were dressed in Abrams security suits just like Jim. The third was evidently a medical technician of some kind. He gave Damon a thorough going over where he lay despite Damon's insistence that he was fine except for the ankle.

"You have a laceration on the back of your head, scratches and cuts on your hands, one of which will need stitches. And you winced when I asked you to turn slightly so I'm guessing bruised ribs."

Jim helped them lift Damon onto the stretcher and then they were on their way to the Lodge where, according to the technician, "we can fix you right up."

Damon had never been in the Lodge before and his perspective at the moment did not give him an immediate appreciation of its grandeur. It had originally been built by Andrew Carnegie, although he was never known to have actually stayed there. The moldings were elaborate, gilded affairs, the two main staircases were marble and mahogany, and the chandeliers – of which he did get an excellent view – were large and elaborate. Unfortunately he only had a fleeting glimpse because they brought him in through the rear entrance.

The guards, now serving as bearers, asked where they should take him. After a momentary hesitation, the technician indicated the dispensary.

"Are you sure?" asked the senior guard. "You know how the old man obsesses about that place."

"It'll be all right. I'll talk to Dr. Wainwright."

Feeling rather foolish, Damon soon found himself lying on an examination table in a sparsely furnished room, most of which was concealed from him by curtains strung from runners attached to the ceiling. He was alone for a moment or two and even managed to sit up before an older man with thick lensed glasses and an irritated look on his face pulled the curtain open and entered.

"So what do we have here?"

"I twisted my ankle while I was hiking. If someone could just drive me home, I'll put ice on it and it'll be okay by morning."

"So you're a doctor, are you?" Damon recoiled from the sarcasm but said nothing. His ankle was examined cursorily by the man he assumed was Dr. Wainwright, who spent even less time with the other injuries. "You're lucky it isn't broken. And we'll have to stitch up your hand."

Damon tried to protest but was ignored. A young woman appeared as though she had been magically summoned bearing a metal pan with gauze and a handful of instruments and there were four stitches in his palm so quickly he almost didn't notice. "If the swelling isn't down by morning, see your own doctor. Someone will be along presently to drive you home." Then Wainwright and the nurse were gone before he could even thank them.

He might have called after them but he caught a glimpse of something on the opposite side of the room when they pulled the curtain back and it froze the words in his throat. It was a young man, hardly more than a boy, and he was lying on an examination table that was the twin of the one upon which Damon lay. Three people hovered over him, two male and one female. They were gowned like doctors in pale green and they wore white plastic gloves, but he could see their faces quite clearly because none of them were masked, which was peculiar because it was obvious even from this angle that the young man's chest had been laid open. Damon could see clamps holding a flap of flesh in place. But what really caught his attention was an abnormally long arm which extended down well past the knee.

There appeared to be two elbows in the arm.

The curtain fell back in place and he could see nothing else, and when the attendants came, they took him out another way and even though he craned his head around, he saw nothing further. They used a wheelchair to bring him to a security van and on the way they passed a uniformed nurse pushing another wheelchair in the opposite direction. This one was also occupied, by a young man who sat with his head slumped and eyes closed, apparently asleep. His face was the same one Damon had seen in the surgery, but his arms were perfectly normal.

He was unusually quiet as they drove him home.

It probably didn't take any longer than normal for Damon's ankle to heal, although it seemed that way to him. As much as he loved his cottage, he hated to be confined to it. His doctor prescribed bed rest and painkillers and suggested hiring someone to prepare his meals for a few days but Damon was obstinate and by the following morning he was hobbling around with a makeshift crutch. A few days later he could manage to put some weight on the ankle and walk almost normally, but he wouldn't be hiking for a while yet. That particularly annoyed him because he wanted to know more about what was going on at the Lodge.

He used his limited social skills to question everyone from Charlie White, whom he called on a flimsy excuse, to the delivery boy who brought the groceries he ordered. The latter was the only one who had any information at all.

"There's people coming and going all the time. I deliver up there four times a week and there's always a full load. There must be thirty or forty people there."

Damon invented a trespasser as an excuse to call Chief Garner, who came up personally. The Chief was one of the most boring people Damon had ever met, but he had decided early on that Damon was a famous person and therefore worthy of special treatment. After relating his fictitious account of a prowler, Damon offered to make coffee and they were soon sitting in his front room. It wasn't hard to turn the conversation to the subject of the Lodge, because the Lodge and its more or less mysterious goings-on had become Boynton's main subject of gossip and speculation.

"Old Van Horn gave me the real lowdown, but he asked me to keep it to myself, so don't go spreading this around. You know about his son's accident, of course."

Damon indicated that this was in fact true. "Paralyzed from the neck down, I understand."

Garner nodded. "No hope, according to the doctors. Too much damage. Can't say that I'd want to live like that, but I don't suppose the boy has any way to end it himself and the old man can't bear the thought of losing him. He' s bringing in some new doctors and trying some new techniques, but that part was too technical for me. I don't suppose there's much chance that it'll do any good, but it can't do any harm and it's bringing some outside money into the town."

Satisfied that he had learned everything that Garner knew, Damon announced that his ankle was starting to hurt and that he needed to lie down for a while and Garner adroitly took the hint.

He was walking normally two days later but the ankle protested if he was upright for too long. It was almost another week before he felt recovered enough to venture out into the nearby woods, but despite the lapse of time he was just as curious about what was happening at the Lodge as he had been on the day of his accident.

His first disappointment was when he approached the perimeter fence and found a strange face looking back at him. Jim had finished his stint and had been rotated to another site. His replacement was a taciturn man with a thin mustache and a suspicious nature. He rebuffed Damon's attempt at an extended conversation.

As it happened, Damon probably knew the area surrounding the Lodge better than anyone else in Boynton. He had spent years exploring every path and near path, had scrambled over rough terrain where neither was available or bulled his way through when thick brush barred the way. He knew of at least two good vantage points from which he could look down into the fenced off area with minimal chance of being spotted in return. It occurred to him to wonder why he thought that should be a concern, but by now he had convinced himself that something was going on at the Lodge that Van Horn and his people did not want anyone else to know.

And he couldn't stop thinking about that elongated arm with the extra joint.

Damon was getting a little too old climb trees but he managed. His knapsack held its usual sandwich and water bottle, but this time he had crammed in a pair of very nice binoculars. Once he had settled into his perch, he did a slow and methodical survey of the Lodge and its environs.

His vantage point was a good one. The modifications had been made to rooms at the rear of the structure, so the wall and windows visible to him almost certainly were the ones in which he was most interested. Sliding glass doors broke a broad expanse of wall into two equal sections, but opaque curtains concealed whatever happened inside. There was a small courtyard and a larger, rather neglected garden. Two paved paths were visible. The one from left to right connected an exterior door to an outbuilding that was apparently now serving as a guard post. Abrams people came and went with some regularity and there was an array of equipment on the roof that suggested it was related to the surveillance cameras mounted along the perimeter. The second path started at the sliding doors, crossed the other diagonally, and extended out toward the perimeter, although Damon could see only the first part of this one. He suspected it was the route by which he had been carried to the Lodge.

He shifted into a less uncomfortable position and settled down to wait.

Damon had never done anything remotely like spying before, but he was a patient, methodical person. He spent most of that first afternoon in the tree, watching people coming and going, making occasional notes in a pad of paper he'd brought with him. There didn't seem to be an obvious pattern and while he did see doctors in green and nurses in white from time to time, often when they stepped outside for a smoke, he never caught a glimpse of any patientss, even when he concentrated on a window whose shades had been pulled open.

The next afternoon it rained, but on the following day he tried his alternative plan. There was a spot atop a rocky ledge that provided a different view of the same general area as well as a swath alongside one wall and down to the front of the Lodge. He would be more exposed there, but it was public land and they couldn't chase him off, although if they spotted him, they'd easily be able to conceal anything they didn't want him to see. He dressed in clothes he thought would match his surroundings and set out, but he had to cut his effort short because the sun was hot overhead and there was no shade. He hadn't seen anything significant.

And so his routine was established. He still produced his daily quota of words – *Murder Comes to Terms* was nearly done – but sometimes he deferred it until the afternoon or even waited until after supper. If the weather looked dubious, he stayed home but it was generally a dry and cheerful June.

Toward the end of the second week, he saw something interesting. Two of the doctors were standing at the glass doors talking and one of them held the door open. Damon had trouble focusing the binoculars, but he peered down over their heads and saw two wheelchairs side by side. Although he couldn't see their faces well, the two patients sitting there both appeared to be young men of approximately the same build and with hair that was identical in color and style. He was pretty sure that the one on the right had an unnaturally long arm but he couldn't be certain. There was something odd about the posture of his companion as well. His chest and shoulders seemed disproportionately large. And then the door closed.

A week passed and he saw nothing else of interest, although he had by now learned to recognize several of the guards and the medical staff. He had even given a few names – Big Hair was a doctor, Slick was one of the senior guards, Gimp was a male nurse who walked with a limp. He could anticipate the shift change at the guard station and he knew who smoked and who did not. The guards and the medical staff rarely interacted except that Slick spent a good deal of time in the latter's domain. Damon never saw any of the other guards enter or exit through the glass doors. They used a smaller entrance right at the limit of his vision.

Damon had been considering abandoning his surveillance the day he saw the fight. He only had a glimpse of it when one of the glass doors shattered. The scene was confused but Damon saw two nurses struggling with a third figure whose face he never saw. They were tangled up together and flailing around on the floor. Slick and another guard responded and blocked his view and two doctors rushed up from the opposite direction. The patient's hospital gown was torn off in the struggle and while Damon never did see his face, he did get a good view of his upper torso. Both arms were the normal length and properly jointed, but they were not attached to the shoulders but to the hips. Damon blinked and looked again just before they all disappeared down a corridor, but he was absolutely certain about what he had seen.

It would be nice to be able to say here that Damon's motives were above reproach, that he was concerned that something unethical if not illegal was taking place, that he believed lives were in jeopardy or that some other great issue demanded his attention. The truth was simply that his curiosity had been aroused to the point where it could no longer be reined in by circumspection.

He would have to get inside the perimeter, undetected, and he was pretty sure he knew how to go about it.

The far side of the lodge was bordered by nearly impassable terrain. Thick brambles, tightly packed trees, and jagged exposed rock formed a natural barrier. The ground was deeply rutted and there were scattered, stagnant pools of water whose surface was almost completely covered by green scum. Mosquitoes and other flying insects thrived there. The security fence had been extended to include this area because it was easier than trying to construct one across it. And there were cameras at strategic locations to make sure no one scaled the fence.

Damon planned to go under it.

During the original construction, there had been plans to turn the rocky, swampy wasteland into a kind of Japanese garden littered with shiny pools. It hadn't taken long before the plan was scrapped as impractical but some initial excavation had been started. There was an old, ruined culvert that ran off to one side. It had been intended as a means of draining excess water and creating a mild current that would have stirred the torpid pools. Part of it had collapsed but it was still passable, although both ends were so heavily overgrown at this time of year that they were undetectable. Damon had walked the area during the winter and he had explored the culvert's full length, so he knew that it ran under the security fence and ended far enough inside that he would not have to worry about the cameras.

He felt a little bit like James Bond as he made his preparations. He would go in at night, of course, and he chose dark clothes that resembled those worn by the guards. No one would be fooled if they got a good look at him but he thought he'd pass from a distance. He had rubber boots to go over his shoes; the passage would be wet and muddy and he could take them off once he was through the passage. His backpack held his camera, a flashlight, pepper spray, and his cell phone. Technically he would be trespassing but if it looked like he was in actual danger, he'd call the police and risk a hefty fine rather than his life. His realization that he thought there might be something there that would justify murder sobered him a bit, but he didn't alter his plans.

The sky was overcast, the moon a thin crescent. He couldn't have asked for better timing.

Negotiating the passage was rather more difficult and time consuming in the dark than in the daylight, and it was also more clogged than he remembered. By the time he reached the egress, his clothing was stained and damp in spots, and there was a tear in one shoulder. Undaunted, he peered around before deciding that he was unobserved, scrambled out, and quickly removed the boots, which made an unpleasant sloshing sound. He heard distant voices briefly and the hum of the air conditioner on the roof, but no one was in sight. Drawing a deep breath, he set off toward the main building.

There was a narrow window at the corner which had been at too sharp an angle to be useful from either of Damon's two observation points. He could see that the curtains were open so he headed directly toward it with an exaggerated caution that would have instantly identified him as an intruder if anyone had spotted him. Fortunately, that didn't happen. Unfortunately, the window didn't show him much. It opened into a small room apparently used for storage. He counted six wheelchairs, all untenanted, and saw several cartons of medical supplies. Damon was about to turn away when it occurred to him to try the window and to his great surprise, he found that it was unlocked.

So far he was guilty of nothing more than trespassing. If he climbed through the window, it would be breaking and entering. He dithered a bit, then decided to find out what else he might accomplish outside before taking the risk. He edged along the side of the building to the corner and froze as he heard the sliding doors move. Then there were two voices, a man and a woman, and the sound of a cigarette lighter.

"I don't understand how we can retrogress in an area we haven't modified," said the woman.

"The matrix is like a piece of woven cloth. Pull a thread in one place and there's a distortion elsewhere. We just have to find a combination that serves our purpose without causing major side effects." The voice was familiar. It was Dr. Wainwright.

"So you're saying we can't ever achieve the goal we've been set? Better not let Van Horn hear you."

"That's not what I'm saying and Mr. Van Horn is well aware of the fact that a perfect solution is beyond our capabilities, at least within the time constraints we're working with."

"I don't think he's entirely sane."

"The father or the son?"

"Either. Both." xx

"That's not our concern. What we're doing here will revolutionize medicine, among other things. We're going to be famous someday, and rich."

"Yeah, if they don't lynch us first."

They were silent after that and Damon waited patiently until he heard the door sliding back and forth again. He peered around the corner carefully but no one was around. A glance at his watch told him that the next shift change at the guard station was still ninety minutes away. He slipped around the side of the building and stopped just short of the sliding doors. The curtains were closed again. He placed his ear against the cold glass but couldn't hear anything.

He made his way along to the point where the other wing of the Lodge extended off to the right. These were the guestrooms that Van Horn had added shortly after purchasing the property. Presumably this is where the off duty guards and the medical staff were staying. The servants' quarters were in a separate structure on the opposite side, at the end of a winding path and concealed by a thick patch of trees. The windows were all on the opposite side, which was almost as well lit as the front entrance itself. Damon didn't dare venture that far so he turned and retraced his steps. Unless something else occurred to him, he would have to try the window.

He had a brief scare when the guard on duty stepped halfway out of his station to look around, but it was boredom rather than suspicion that motivated him and he quickly returned to his post without spotting Damon, who was in plain view. Catching his breath, Damon moved quickly along the line of the building and returned to the window. There was no light on in the inner room but the door was cracked open so Damon could see quite well. He eased the window up slowly – it made almost no sound at all – and awkwardly pushed his upper body inside, ascertained that there was nothing within range that would topple over with a crash if jostled, and then made an undignified entrance by crawling down the inner wall.

He peered around the door jamb, trying to orient himself. He could see privacy curtains to his left and he was pretty sure that was where the doctor had examined his ankle. An empty passageway to the right curved around toward the glass door. Damon heard some slight sounds of movement but no voices. He decided that nothing was to be gained by waiting so he slipped out through the door, heart racing, wondering if this had been such a good idea after all. But now that he was committed, he was determined not to retreat without having learned something.

Trying not to make a sound, he crossed to the nearest of the curtains. He was pretty sure that the space just beyond was empty and a surreptitious glance confirmed it. Once past the curtain, he was more confident than ever that this was the examination table upon which he'd been placed, which meant that the other one should be directly opposite. He moved to the opposite end of the curtain and peered around just in time to see a young man with a ponytail wearing a nurse's uniform stride past. He pulled his head in quickly, but the passerby had his eyes turned away and had seen nothing.

Damon waited a few seconds before emerging, nodded when he saw the second examination table, and then turned to follow the nurse.

Within a few steps he reached an archway blocked by yet another curtain, and he could hear the murmur of voices from someplace beyond. A hasty look showed a clear field ahead and he passed through this as well, made a sharp right turn, and found himself looking into what appeared to be hospital ward with a half dozen beds to his left, a bewildering array of electronics and unidentifiable equipment to his right. There were two large glass walled boxes that looked like telephone booths and a squat cubical metal tank approximately six wide and deep and perhaps five feet high. There was a large indentation in the top with a heavy handle affixed.

More significantly, five of the six beds were occupied. Damon tried to determine whether any of the patients had an oversized arm but their limbs were not all visible. He did identify one whose shoulders seemed to be in the wrong position, but even this one was covered by a blanket. He wanted pictures as evidence that he wasn't seeing things and to get them he'd have to go closer. The problem with that was that two doctors were in the room, not far from the beds, speaking softly. Damon guessed they were the same two who had gone outside a few minutes earlier.

He was growing increasingly frustrated when they turned in unison and walked over to one of the beds. The woman carefully pulled down the blanket covering the sleeping – or drugged – patient and Damon saw nothing unusual except that the hips were narrow. Very narrow, in fact. It didn't seem possible that they could support the normal sized legs attached to them.

There were more words he couldn't hear, then the blanket was pulled back up. The two turned away and disappeared into a passageway that Damon couldn't see. Realizing this might be his only chance, he took out his camera and cautiously emerged from cover.

As he drew closer, he spotted the anomalies. One had a withered arm, another a disproportionately small torso. All five were alive but unconscious; he could see the rise and fall of their chests, although in one case it looked as though the chest expanded to either side rather than forward and upward. What really caught his attention, however, were their faces. They were all young men. In fact, they were all the same young man. And Damon had a very good idea who they were. In some unimaginable way, these were all variations of Peter Van Horn, and Damon immediately had a theory to explain everything. They were cloning him, which was very illegal and which justified the secrecy and the security.

It was a very satisfying and plausible explanation, but of course it was entirely untrue.

He remembered the camera and raised it to take a picture and that's when he heard a voice behind him. Half turning, he recognized Slick and also realized that, as his fictional detective was always saying, the jig was up.

Damon sat for several minutes in a small office with only a single door. He was alone and as far as he knew the door was unlocked, but he was quite sure that someone was standing outside to prevent him from leaving. Eventually the door opened and he saw Slick, but the security man stepped aside and a much older man entered. Damon got to his feet.

"Good evening, Mr. Van Horn." He extended his hand, but it was ignored.

"You're the writer, aren't you?"

"I'm afraid so. I wanted to try something surreptitious and adventurous to get the right atmosphere for the book I'm writing. Sneaking in here was a bit foolish though, I admit."

"Don't waste my time, Mr. Sanders. You've been watching us for weeks. I'd have chased you off except I thought that would just draw more attention to this place. Your daring little adventure has presented us with a serious problem. Both of us, you understand."

Damon declined to say anything.

"Just how much do you know? Or think you know?"

Damon considered pleading nearly complete ignorance, but he didn't think he'd be able to fool Van Horn. His gaze pressed against Damon like an almost physical force. "I know that you have several deformed versions of your son here. I assume you're conducting illegal research into cloning."

"Cloning? Actually that's not a bad deduction. I looked into the technology. It has promise but not for a long time yet, probably not during our lifetimes. No, we aren't doing cloning. Our experiments are technically not illegal. They involve an entirely new technology and there are no applicable laws to hinder us. But some of the things we must do would strike the general public as unsavory at best. I am a desperate and determined man, Mr. Sanders. The doctors have told me that the damage to Peter is irreversible, that he will never move his limbs again. I've never allowed myself to be ruled by the opinions of others and I will live to see them proven wrong."

Van Horn's insistence that they were not experimenting with cloning had stunned Damon, who could think of no other explanation. "But I saw them," he protested. "Five of them."

"Are we back up to five?" Van Horn seemed to be talking to himself. "I thought we had finished the dissections. It's sometimes hard to keep track." He shook his head. "That's not important. What am I to do with you?"

"You could show me to the door and wish me a good evening."

"Don't be naïve."

"You mean to have me arrested then?" He felt relief rather than shame at the prospect.

"That wouldn't help either of us. You'd be out on bail tomorrow and free to tell people what you've seen. There would be questions, investigations, and even though we have broken no laws, there would be delays. No, I'm afraid you'll have to be our guest for a while."

"Your prisoner is what you mean."

"We're all prisoners of something, Mr. Sanders. You'll be well taken care of."

"What if I decide to leave anyway?" His knapsack had been taken from him, along with his phone.

"I think we can prevent that. But let's talk of something more pleasant. What if I provided you with an incentive to stay voluntarily?"

"What kind of incentive did you have in mind?"

Van Horn rubbed his hands together. "We're making history here, sir. It never occurred to me until now that there should be some sort of official record kept. These scientists and doctors keep notes, of course, but I had something more informal in mind, something that would convey to the layman the excitement and importance of what we're accomplishing."

"And what would that be?"

Van Horn was silent a moment. "No, I can't explain it that easily. I'll have to show you. Come with me." He started for the door and Damon, after a momentary hesitation, moved to follow him. On the threshold, Van Horn turned back. "Don't be fooled by appearances. I haven't had them handcuff you but you'll be watched closely at all times and you'll find it harder to get out than it was getting in."

Damon followed mutely and soon found himself in a large, comfortably furnished room with a fireplace at one end. Despite the heat, a fire had been set and beside it sat, or rather slumped, Peter Van Horn in an elaborate wheelchair. His eyes were open and they may have moved slightly when the two men entered, but the interest was fleeting.

"Because of his poor circulation, he's always cold. And he has declined dramatically since we started this program." There was genuine tragedy in Van Horn's voice now. "Peter was a lovely boy. He's everything to me now that his mother is gone. I won't allow him to follow her."

Damon could think of nothing adequate to say.

"The doctors insist that there is nothing more to do but maintenance, that we don't have the knowledge required to repair his body. In the strictest sense, I suppose, they're absolutely correct. But I have made a career of bypassing immovable obstacles. I heard rumors of a new technology, rumors that sounded absurd and which were not taken seriously. To be fair, I considered it nonsense myself, but I was desperate by then and anything remotely promising was worth investigating. And to my surprise, I found out that the rumors were, if anything, understated."

From there Damon was led to a small room devoid of conventional furniture but nearly filled with devices he could not identify including two glass lined booths similar to the ones he had seen earlier. "This is the original equipment used to develop the process. We have improved some of the auxiliaries but have not touched most of the hardware." He touched a master switch and several of the devices powered up. "Do you have some personal item that I might borrow for a demonstration?"

"Your security people emptied my pockets, I'm afraid. They even took my watch."

Van Horn sighed, then picked up a pad and pencil from the desk. "Write something on the top sheet, then fold it in half so that I can't see it."

Puzzled but curious, Damon inscribed the words "accept no substitute", tore off the page, and folded it as requested. Van Horn opened the door to one of the glass chambers. "No, don't give it to me. Place it inside."

Damon did so. Van Horn closed the door, turned to a panel of electronics, nodded to himself, and pressed a button. There was the faintest of hums. "Operation of the equipment is absurdly simple. Please open the door to the other chamber and see what's inside."

There was a folded piece of paper on the floor and it bore the same words Damon had just written. "Neat trick," he said and turned. Van Horn handed him a second piece of paper. "Here's the one you actually wrote."

They were, insofar as Damon could tell, identical.

"Are you telling me you can duplicate matter?"

Van Horn shook his head. "No, not really. But we can rearrange existing matter into specified configurations." He rapped his hand against a small metal tank. "As long as there is an adequate supply of each element found in the original, the machine can create an exact duplicate. The raw materials must be replenished, of course. There is no violation of the law of conservation of mass and energy."

Damon remained skeptical. "Even if that's true, how does it help your situation?"

"It doesn't, not directly. And this primitive equipment actually doesn't make very good copies, particularly of living things. The scanner is accurate insofar as we can determine but the reassembled copies invariably contain errors. They're too subtle to be noticeable with most inanimate objects, but if we used this to reproduce a rabbit, for example, it would almost certainly die within days or weeks."

Damon made an intuitive leap. "Are you telling me that those poor boys I saw in the ward upstairs were created by this machine?"

Van Horn shook his head vigorously. "Of course, but we're not monsters here. We didn't use human subjects until we were quite sure that the replication process was accurate enough to produce viable copies."

"They didn't look particularly viable to me. I'd say you still have a lot of work to do."

"Oh, but those poor souls weren't the result of poor replication. I told you, we've advanced to the point where those flaws are minimal. The anomalies you saw were, well, not quite deliberate, but the results of our interference with the normal process."

"I don't follow."

Van Horn smiled. "The scan is data, Mr. Sanders, and data can be manipulated. If an original scan is altered, the reassembly will reflect those changes." He sighed. "Unfortunately our understanding of how that data works is less than perfect. Far less. It's not quite trial and error but there is an element of chance involved. We make an edit, produce our output, and then examine the results in order to plot the course of cause and effect. Given enough time we might even be able to dispense with the initial scan entirely and just create scripts designed to produce whatever we want, but none of us will live to see that day. My goal here is considerably less grandiose."

"Just what is that goal?" But Damon already had a suspicion.

"I want to cure my son, Mr. Sanders. Restore him to full health or at least some reasonable semblance. His injuries were severe and we've been trying to resolve them individually. If we can reconfigure his profile so that the crushed portion of his spine is whole again, then it is possible that he might walk some day. A restored kidney would free him from dialysis." He raised his hands placatingly. "Oh, I'm not unrealistic. I don't expect miracles. Well, actually, I do expect miracles but not perfect ones. Nevertheless I intend to see Peter leave his wheelchair behind and lead something approximating a normal life before I die. This is his only chance."

"But what about the others? The copies."

"We study them. We examine the physical changes inside their bodies and use what we learn to revise the next version."

"But what happens to them? How do you tell the world that there are a half dozen versions of your son around?"

"But there won't be. We've reassembled dozens of them, as a matter of fact. Some died within a few minutes, you understand, and some were in terrible pain and were terminated immediately. The more promising ones are interviewed by our psychologists -- we need a sound mind as well as a sound body. Eventually they will all be recycled."

Damon was appalled. "That's murder!"

Van Horn shook his head. "Neither legally nor morally. They have no legal existence as human beings. They are distorted shadows of my son. We create them and then we uncreate them, if you will."

"I doubt the courts will agree with your interpretation."

Van Horn smiled. "Let us suppose that I were to be indicted for the murder of Peter 87. I would simply instruct my staff to call up the scan of Peter 87 and reassemble him, thus depriving the prosecutor of a victim. They're not dead, really. They're just on hiatus."

Damon was convinced that Van Horn was insane and almost said so, but discretion stilled his tongue. "This is all very hard to believe."

"I completely understand. As long as you are going to be our guest, perhaps you would like to see the process for yourself?"

Uncertain, Damon nodded slightly.

"Very good. We're trying a new matrix tomorrow. I will send someone for you at the appropriate time." A security guard appeared at the door. Van Horn must have summoned him with a silent pager. "Simon here will see you to your room. Good night, Mr. Sanders. And please reserve your judgment until you know the entire story."

Despite having been confined in quite a nice room, Damon had an uneasy night. He woke the following morning greatly disoriented -- it had been more than a decade since he had last waked up in a bed other than his own. He realized that he was under some form of surveillance when breakfast was delivered promptly upon his awakening, but he had little appetite. A change of clothing was also provided. A woman wearing security garb arrived a short while later and conducted him to the library, where he was "requested" to wait until Van Horn called for him. He amused himself scanning the titles of the books, but his attention wandered.

Van Horn summoned him at mid-morning. The guard led him to the room he'd peered into the night before. Van Horn, the doctor Damon had dubbed Big Hair, and a technician he hadn't seen before stood in front of an array of equipment that vaguely resembled the setup where Van Horn had demonstrated the replication process. To one side there was a jumble of boxes, various electronics he didn't recognize, a large red toolbox, some sections of sheetrock obviously intended to cover one wall where the wiring was still exposed, and other debris. Two canvas tarps had been draped so that they partially concealed the tangle.

To one side, one of the Peters sat in a wheelchair. He had an oversized chest and, Damon now realized, disproportionately large arms as well, giving him something of an apelike appearance. His head was down on his chest but Damon sensed that he was awake and alert. A female nurse stood beside him.

Van Horn greeted Damon and his escort left without a word. "I promised to show you the process in action. I feel certain we won't shock your sensibilities just yet. This is merely a routine scan for our database. May I introduce Dr. Curtain, second in command to Dr. Wainwright, our head of research."

Damon reluctantly shook hands. Dr. Curtain didn't look any better pleased than he, but probably for very different reasons.

"Let's get this done," she said firmly.

The nurse took one of the Peter's oversized arms and helped him stand up. "As you can see," said Van Horn, "we have progressed considerably with the mobility problem. This Peter," he hesitated and turned to Curtain. "Which one is he?"

"237. He's our most recent output. The interview has been completed so as soon as we have a valid scan, he can go to surgery for internal examination."

Damon noticed Curtain's perhaps unconscious effort to dehumanize this iteration of Peter but he didn't say anything.

Van Horn took up the thread. "Unfortunately, as you can see, there was an unforeseen change to the upper torso. We haven't been able to plot all of the interrelationships yet. Fortunately we have had other subjects far closer to normal. We'll superimpose the relevant portion of that profile on 237's scan, try to reconcile the broken connections, and generate 238 in a few days. Although we've had some setbacks, we've generally been moving closer to our goal."

Damon felt a surge of dull anger. "Assuming that you manufacture a son you find acceptable, what happens to the original?"

Van Horn seemed taken aback, as though he had never really considered the issue before. "I'll make suitable provision for his maintenance."

"Why not just process his body for the raw materials?" Damon asked flatly. "After all, if you get what you want, he won't really be your son any longer, will he?"

Van Horn looked momentarily furious but he quickly regained control. "That really is none of your concern, Mr. Sanders." He turned to Curtain. "Let's proceed, shall we?"

The Peter was led to the first of the glass booths where he docilely stepped inside. The technician hovered over a control panel, there was a rise in the background noise, and then the sound dropped back after perhaps thirty seconds. The nurse opened the door and began to help Peter out.

That's when things went very wrong. The nurse had just leaned in toward the Peter as though to offer her hand when the latter turned and swung one oversized arm like a club. The young woman toppled away from him without a sound, literally knocked off her feet, and fell heavily to the floor. The technician started forward uncertainly and the Peter charged, rather unsteadily, and locked his arms around his opponent.

Damon missed most of what happened next because he instinctively stepped backward, caught his ankle in a coil of copper wire, and crashed into a stack of wooden crates. He saw the pile wobble and tried to roll away, but it was too late. There was excruciating pain as one of the boxes dropped onto his foot and lower leg. For a few seconds, he saw and heard nothing, experienced only a wave of burning agony. This time, it turned out, he really had broken his ankle.

The pain didn't go away but it seemed to lessen some after a moment, enough so that Damon regained his interest in his surroundings. He raised his head and immediately saw Peter 237, who stood facing away from him, slightly bent over. As Damon watched, Peter lifted Dr. Curtain's limp form and threw her over his shoulder. He walked directly to the large metal tank with the hatchway and opened it. He had no difficulty in pushing the inert body through the opening. As he closed the hatch, a display screen illuminated to show a bar graph whose readings began to rise almost at once.

Damon tried to move and there was a fresh rush of pain from his ankle, but he ignored it as best he could and half crawled, half rolled behind some of the debris. From this vantage point he could see Arthur Van Horn lying motionless on his back. There was no sign of the technician or the nurse. He cringed when the Peter turned around, but it was Van Horn that the replicant was interested in. When he leaned down to pick up his father's inert form – assuming that the father/son relationship was an accurate description – Damon took advantage of his inattention to lift the edge of one of the tarps and slide behind the sheetrock. It wasn't much in the way of concealment but it was the best he could manage.

He felt a touch of bitter irony when Van Horn's body went into the hopper.

The Peter was standing in front of another display now and lines of data began to scroll upward. One line highlighted when the Peter selected it, and a second later there was a loud hum. The glass walls of the second booth misted over, then slowly began to clear. Peter 237 opened the door and a very similar figure emerged. In fact, it was another Peter 237, identical in every detail insofar as Damon could determine. There was now a Peter 238.

They closed the door and returned to the control panel. Two minutes later a Peter 239 had joined them and, after the same interval, a fourth. When the fifth emerged, a green light at the top left hand corner of the screen turned red. The Peters conferred but Damon could not hear what they were saying. Then three of them abruptly turned and walked away while the other two stood immobile.

The threesome came back after less than five minutes, half dragging, half carrying a woman whose face Damon never saw. She went into the hopper screaming and a few minutes later there were six Peters. Four of them left then and after a slightly longer interval they returned with two inert forms, both male, one a security guard.

The pattern continued for a couple of hours while Damon remained hidden, terrified that they would notice him. The pain in his ankle waxed and waned and he might even have lost consciousness briefly once or twice. In any case, he lost count and had no idea how many iterations of Peter 237 were not out and about, but he guessed at least a score. He heard shouting once or twice, and a gun went off somewhere distant, but the conversion operation continued unabated for at least an hour. They had finally stopped throwing bodies into the hopper and the indicator glowed red. Perhaps they had run out of people to process for their raw material. Damon estimated that around forty people had been working at the Lodge. Did that mean that there were now a like number of malformed Peters at large?

The crowd thinned out and at one point there were no Peters within sight. Damon took advantage of this to improve his concealment and was confident that unless they actually set out to search the area, they would not find him. Or at least as confident as he could be under the circumstances. He had heard virtually no conversation among them; they seemed to know what they were to do without any central direction or planning That made sense, he realized, because they were all of the same mind, literally.

He thought about sneaking back to the storage room and leaving through the window, but he wasn't sure if he could manage it with only one functioning ankle, and to be perfectly honest he was so frightened that he just wanted to curl up where he was. Nor was there much opportunity to attempt an escape. Except for two brief periods, there was always at least one Peter in the room with him, and usually two or three.

Since the security people had taken his wristwatch, Damon had no way of judging the passage of time, but he guessed it was early afternoon when a large party of Peters returned to the room. With them were a half dozen other people, all of them conscious this time. At least three of the Peters were armed, weapons presumably taken from the security detail. The newcomers were all variously arguing or protesting, but they didn't resist physically until the Peters began shooting. Damon recognized Norm Palmer and some of the other faces were familiar, but he stayed quietly where he lay while they were systematically killed and dropped into the hopper.

More Peters emerged.

Two more batches were processed similarly before the external gunfire started. There were no new victims after that. The sounds of battle rose and fell sporadically for some time. Damon found himself alone again and this time he was determined to make his escape. He found a broom in one corner and turned it into a makeshift crutch. The shooting seemed to be underway at the front and along one side of the complex. The window through which he'd entered was on the opposite side.

Hobbling painfully, he made his way down the corridor and into the room. He tossed the broom outside and then crawled through, crying out sharply as his ankle brushed across the sill. His landing was undignified and he was badly winded, but at least he was out of the building.

There was shouting not far away and the level of gunfire was increasing. The faintest odor of tear gas reached him as well. He tried to prop himself up with the broom, but it was useless on the rough ground here and he ended up crawling slowly and painfully away from the building. Everything looked different from this perspective and he was afraid he was going the wrong way, but eventually he spotted the entrance to the culvert and pulled himself inside. That was as far as his strength could take him, however, and he promptly passed out.

He was feverish and incoherent when a search party heard his moaning and found him several hours later. Damon had no memory of that part of his adventure at all. He was taken to the Boynton Emergency Room and patched up, then slept for most of the next day. When he next opened his eyes, there was a police officer waiting to take his statement. Damon was cooperative but became testy when the officer refused to answer his own questions and it wasn't until the following day that he learned what had happened.

Besieged by the state and local police, the Peters had set fire to the Lodge. Most of the building, including the laboratory and medical sections, had been destroyed. None of the Peters – including the original – had survived. No members of the staff had survived except Dr. Wainwright, who had been away from the site at the time. Two security officers who had been on perimeter patrol were still alive but they knew almost nothing about what had happened. Damon was, essentially, the only remaining witness.

He was never sure whether or not they believed his story. The authorities were invariably polite and rarely openly skeptical. If they did accept his word, they weren't about to admit it. The official story was that Arthur Van Horn had become involved with some apocalyptic cult after losing his wife and seeing his only son crippled for life. The cult members, who had all dressed identically, had perished either of gunshot wounds or in the fire. None of them were ever identified by name.

Damon knew that much of this was nonsense, but saw no purpose in contradicting the official story. Anything he said would be explained away as delusion resulting from his traumatic experiences. The only people who would take him seriously were people whom he could not take seriously.

He was tempted by his experience to conclude that there really was some knowledge which humanity should not possess, or at least not yet, but as time passed he decided that wasn't true. The fact was that no matter how wonderful and promising a new piece of knowledge might be, there were always a few people who would pervert it into a destructive monstrosity. People like Arthur Van Horn would see only what they wanted to see, and the consequences for others were inconsequential.

Damon was consoled by the fact that in their death throes, the Peters had destroyed the technology which had created them. Perhaps, he told himself, we'll be a little wiser the next time around.

Because of his broken ankle, Damon didn't leave his house for almost a month, and because of that confinement, he never saw the unmarked trucks and the crew who picked through the rubble of the Lodge and, every so often, carried out something to be loaded and taken away.

Part 5: KNOCKOFFS

Dr. Eric Wainwright did not deal with frustration well, even though he had had a great deal of practice recently. He glared balefully at the apparatus arranged on the table in his basement work room and ran one hand through thinning hair. As far as he could tell, everything corresponded to the specifications he'd retrieved from the backup copy of his files but there had been gaps, things he had forgotten to save, data developed by his colleagues that had not made it into the official record. All of that was lost in the fire, of course, along with all of his former colleagues and any information that had rested in their minds.

He tried to initiate the reassembly process one more time. As before the glass dome clouded as the appropriate elements were drawn from the storage banks and sprayed into the enclosed environment. There was a kind of swirling as though something was trying to take form, but when it cleared there were simply some featureless lumps of matter where there should have been a copy of his Rolex, which for some reason had refused to run shortly after he had begun this round of experiments. Swearing softly, and uncharacteristically, he turned to the console and shut everything down, then cleaned out the reassembly chamber and dropped the formless residue into the hopper to be recycled.

Wainwright went back upstairs and tried to put the project out of his mind. Either he would figure it out and become possibly the wealthiest person in human history, or he wouldn't figure it out and at the end of his sabbatical he would return to Brown and resume his half hearted effort to siphon knowledge into student brains. No pressure at all.

The prospect of cooking dinner didn't appeal to him and he was about to go out for lunch when the telephone rang. One of his few concessions to tradition was that he still had a landline. He spent most of his day working with computers and electronics so he tried to avoid them as much as possible in his off time, although he had a spiffy cell phone as well.

"Dr. Wainwright? This is Dave Geller. We've made some progress on that matter you referred to us and I was wondering if I could stop by this afternoon."

"Have you located the elusive lady?"

"That's a complicated question, sir. I have some surveillance photographs for you to look at. And some of the details are not the kind of thing I would discuss over the phone."

Wainwright glanced at his wristwatch – a new one, not the Rolex. "What time did you have in mind?"

"About two or a little after."

"I'll be expecting you."

He tried to put the whole matter out of his mind and enjoy lunch, but on the way home from the diner he realized that he couldn't remember what he had just eaten. If only Van Horn had listened to him and imposed stricter controls, things would not have gotten out of hand. They had been making good progress. Gupta had a brilliant mind and a gift for analyzing intricate arrays of data, and Gobel was a wizard with electronics and had made several small but definite improvements in the hardware design. All that intellect, experience, and talent was gone now. He was the only survivor from the disaster in Boynton other than a few of the security guards. Wainwright still didn't know exactly what had gone wrong, but apparently some of the experimental subjects had gotten out of control, had massacred the staff, and set fire to the building during a firefight with the authorities.

Geller showed up right on time. Unlike the diminutive Wainwright, he was a big man, well over six feet, with unruly hair, a jaw line that would always look as though he needed a shave, and the arms of a lumberjack. He declined Wainwright's offer of a beer – which was just as well because he'd forgotten to replenish his stock – and took a seat in the living room, dropping several file folders onto the coffee table.

"You've made some progress?" prompted Wainwright hopefully.

"We think so, but there are some unusual aspects to the case. You never specified why you wanted us to track down this woman and that's not unusual in this business, but do you mind if I ask the question?"

Wainwright considered his response. His work with Van Horn had taught him caution. "Laurie Kaitan, later Laurie Carter, was engaged in research similar to my own at the time of her alleged death. If she is really dead, I would be interested in any papers or equipment she may have left behind. If she is alive, then I hope to approach her directly and suggest collaboration. But in the latter case, discretion is necessary. She must have had a reason to fake her own death and it's not likely that she will be overjoyed to find out that her ruse has been discovered."

"Pardon me for asking, but is this project of yours legal? Could she have gone underground to avoid arrest?"

Wainwright looked him straight in the eyes. "To the best of my knowledge, there is nothing in this line of research that is a violation of any existing laws. It is quite revolutionary, however."

"And dangerous, I assume."

"Why do you say that?"

"Dr. Wainwright, we conduct a routine check on all of our clients. We are aware of your connection to the unfortunate events in New York."

"It's no secret that I was working there as a consultant, but I signed a nondisclosure agreement and in any case I was traveling when the tragedy occurred. I know no more than you do about what happened that day." His eyes drifted away as he lied. Geller certainly knew that he was being less than candid but Wainwright didn't care. He was hired help.

"Laurie Carter is legally dead as well."

"An accident, I understand. But as you know, I think there was an error in identification. I believe she is still alive. "

"The husband would have to have been an accomplice. He identified the body."

"Naturally."

"And the husband is also deceased, killed in a fire along with two still unidentified females."

"So you have told me. But the date of this tragedy suggests that neither of the two were the woman I am looking for."

Geller was silent for a moment, then picked up one of the folders and slid out the black and white headshot of a young woman. "This is a blowup of Laurie Kaitan's high school yearbook picture." Wainwright took it and Geller produced a second. "And this is the notice of her engagement." The woman looked slightly older and the quality of the photograph wasn't great, but they were clearly the same woman. "And this is a snapshot her brother-in-law took during a visit." The third picture was in color. Long hair brushed her shoulders as she sat at a wooden picnic table, but she didn't look as though she was enjoying herself.

Geller discarded the folder and picked up another. "Take a look at this."

The first photograph – obviously taken from a distance and without the subject's knowledge – showed a woman standing at a mailbox. Her expression was grim, almost angry, and her long hair was tied in a pony tail.

"That looks like her. When was this taken?" Wainwright felt a rush of excitement.

"A few days ago. Here's another."

It was roughly the same setting but the subject was descending the porch steps. Neither shot showed much of the house but what Wainwright could see looked run down. It was unquestionably the same woman, except that her hair was in braids and she was wearing a different blouse and jeans.

"Is this where she's living now?"

But Geller didn't answer. Instead he proffered a third photograph. The woman in braids was on the porch again, this time back toward the shadowy end. She was talking – apparently with considerable animation – to another woman who could be seen only in profile but whose face was quite recognizable. It was Laurie Kaitan/Carter with a ponytail. They were both Laurie Kaitan/Carter.

Wainwright realized the implications immediately and tried to keep his face impassive, but he didn't completely succeed.

"You don't look particularly surprised."

"Very little surprises me, Mr. Geller."

"My first reaction was to assume they were twins, possibly even triplets. That would explain the misidentification after Laurie Carter's accidental death. But we checked the birth records. She was an only child. The records could have been altered, of course, but that seemed unlikely. Perhaps you have an alternate explanation?"

Wainwright knew perfectly well what the explanation was, but he was not about to reveal it. "Our mutual research involves a process that makes it possible to simulate the appearance of another person quite closely. Farther than that I'm afraid I'm not willing to go."

"You're the boss. Anyway, we watched the place for three days. It was rented by someone named Laura Kelly about two months ago. She and her roommate – name unknown – have kept pretty much to themselves. None of the neighbors seem to know them. We managed to get a copy of her references from the landlord. They're bogus. He never checks. They paid the damage deposit and first two months rent in cash, used a postal money order this month. They may have cell phones but there is no land line. One of them – the one in the ponytail – goes out a lot at night, alone. Her friend has not left the house since we started watching, unless they're switching hairstyles to fool anyone watching. The one with the ponytail has bad posture, walks with a slight stoop."

"Where is the house?"

"Central Falls." Geller took the third folder. "Here's a summary of all the information we've gathered, the address, etc. If you want us to follow the subjects, we can do that for an additional fee. Are you satisfied that we have found the person you were looking for – whoever she is?"

"Yes. That's all for now. Send me your bill. I'm quite happy with the results.

It had been pure chance that had set Wainwright on the trail. Van Horn provided the initial stimulus. He had learned that the late Laurie Carter's fingerprints had been found at a crime scene, a home invasion that included a double homicide. The computer had matched it to the prints taken when she had applied for a security clearance to work as an intern at a defense contractor. The police had been puzzled but eventually concluded that Carter must have visited the deceased at some time prior to her death. She and her husband had lived only a ten minute walk away so that was entirely plausible. The crime lab had insisted that the prints were recent but since that was obviously impossible, they had been ignored.

Unfortunately this had all occurred only a few days before the disaster in Boynton. If Van Horn had initiated any inquiries, he had not mentioned it to Wainwright. Van Horn was not easily distracted from his main purpose, and it was possible, even probable, that he had never gotten around to it.

Wainwright pondered the problem. He didn't know whether one of the two women in the photographs was the original or if they were both copies. If it was the latter case, he was dubious about their ability to help. The imperfections in the reassembly process were mentioned in the documentation Van Horn had obtained, and they had witnessed the same deterioration during their experiments. Wainwright had privately believed that Van Horn was doomed to failure. The scanning operation was so complex that even if they had succeeded in correcting his son's gross physical problems, they would almost certainly have introduced other faults, perhaps undetectable ones. The human intellect was particularly fragile. Whatever the result might have been, no matter how closely it resembled the younger Van Horn, it would not have been his son.

He would have to find out whether or not the two women could help him directly, and whether or not they had access to other documentation or even equipment that had not been destroyed in the fire. At the same time, he needed to be cautious. One of the Lauries had almost certainly murdered her husband in order to preserve the secret, and Wainwright had no desire to perish in another "accident." He would have to be circumspect.

That afternoon, Wainwright rented a post office box. Using that as the return address, he mailed a letter addressed to "Laurie Carter, care of 234 Madison Road" in Central Falls. He didn't return to his workroom that evening.

A week passed with no reply. Wainwright made some slight progress with the reassembler. The blobs of matter now at least took the shape of his castoff Rolex. He created multiple new scans and tried them, but there was no discernible improvement. The crystal in the watch was now translucent and he thoughtfully made a note in his journal that the scanning process was not without its hazards. He was unable to determine whether this resulted from his own error in building the device or whether it was inherent in the process. None of the paperwork that he had seen referred to it and he had no examples to compare with his own work.

On the eighth day after mailing the letter, Wainwright was considering a physical confrontation when he found a response in his box at the post office. He didn't open it there, but took it home, conscious of the fact that this might be a turning point.

There was a single piece of paper inside and one line of not particularly neat hand writing. "Come to the house Friday at 6." There was no signature.

Wainwright was not a particularly brave man. Nor was he stupid. He had no intention of walking unprotected into obvious danger. At the same time, he was determined to find out if the two women could help him. He was also curious about their survival and circumstances, but this was largely incidental. He could live with continued ignorance so long as they helped him advance toward his goal. Their secret was safe with him unless it proved advantageous to reveal it.

That Friday, shortly before six o'clock, Wainwright sat in his car watching 234 Madison, and he had a small handgun in his coat pocket. The house was even less appealing than it appeared in the photograph. The grass grew in unruly patches in the small yard, several trees brushed the walls with their branches, there were tiles missing from the roof, and the paint was dry and peeling. The ancient Volkswagen in the driveway wasn't much better. There were visible dents and rust spots. He had been parked across the street for almost half an hour but hadn't seen any sign that anyone was home.

Gathering his courage, he got out and walked slowly across the street and across to the porch. The doorbell was hanging loose so he knocked, then stepped back. When the door opened, he saw a woman with a ponytail standing there, and she matched the photographs Geller had shown him.

"I assume you're one of the Laurie Carters." He made no effort to go inside.

There was an uncomfortable pause. "I don't know what you're talking about."

Wainwright took a photograph out of his pocket. It was a snapshot of the experimental apparatus in his workroom. He handed it to the woman and she obviously recognized what it was. "Is this supposed to mean something to me?"

"I think it's of mutual interest and we should probably talk about it."

After a second she nodded. "All right. C'mon in."

Wainwright didn't budge. "It's a nice day. Why don't we sit out on your porch until we get to know each other better?"

The woman turned to look behind her. "We'll be out on the porch, Seven." She stepped outside and closed the door behind her.

There were two fraying wicker chairs and they sat facing each other. "And what should I call you?" asked Wainwright. "I've already told you my name."

"You can call me Laurie."

Wainwright nodded. "But you're not the original are you?"

She remained silent for a few seconds. "I was number three, but I'm senior now. What do you want?"

"I've been working on Carl Wrentham's discovery, just as you were. Progress has been slower than I expected and I was hoping that you might be able to help me out." He glanced across the front of the house with an expression of distaste. "I gather that you and your friend lack the resources to pursue the research on your own. It is possible that we might be of mutual assistance to each other."

Laurie looked at the photograph again. "This is based on an early configuration."

"I had access to Wrentham's original journals and some of his niece's notes, but some of the materials were obviously incomplete."

"Your reassembler looks primitive, but I can't really tell from this. You say you have money?"

"I have enough. What do you have to offer if we become partners?"

She stood up abruptly. "Come with me." Wainwright hesitated, then mentally shrugged. He would have to take the chance sooner or later. With one hand in his pocket and next to his weapon, he followed her into the house.

The interior was, if anything, worse than the outside. The plaster was cracked, wall paper hung loose, the carpet was filthy, furniture broken down, and above all else it smelled bad – stale and sour. He followed Laurie upstairs to one of the bedrooms, which had been stripped of its furniture. In its place was an array of equipment that looked very much like the setup in his workroom, except that it was on a smaller scale. There was a computer workstation at one end.

"Does it work?" The question erupted involuntarily.

"Mostly. We never did eliminate the reassembly errors. I don't suppose you've solved that, have you?"

Wainwright was not about to admit that his reassembler barely worked at all. "Show me."

The other Laurie, Seven, came into the room. Her hair had been let down but she was almost certainly the one pictured in braids. They could have been twins, obviously, although Seven was bent forward slightly, as though her back was giving her trouble. She didn't say anything and Laurie ignored her.

"Got any cash on you?"

Wainwright took out his wallet and handed her a fifty. She placed it in one of the two domes and pressed a key on the workstation. There was a very faint hum and then a green light came on. Laurie nodded to herself, typed in a few characters, and the second chamber began to glow, then grew misty. The process took longer than Wainwright expected but at the end there was a second fifty dollar bill in the second chamber. When he looked it over, he could detect no flaw.

"It looks okay to me."

"First copy," said Laurie. "Sometimes we get three passable ones before the errors become visible. Then we have to swap it for fresh currency and start over. It takes a lot of effort to generate a few thousand dollars."

He went closer and peered at the setup. "How did you set this all up?"

"This was our pilot project, back when we had the lab in the barn. We needed the space so this was moved to a storage locker and wasn't destroyed in the fire."

"Do you have the schematics and logs?"

She shook her head. "Nothing like that. What you see is what we have."

Wainwright felt a rush of disappointment but also excitement. The documentation would have been wonderful, but a working model was nearly as satisfying. He was still considering the possibilities when something was jammed against his back.

"That's a gun Seven is holding. She has problems of self control so I wouldn't do anything that might anger or frighten her."

Wainwright chose his words carefully. "I came here to offer you a partnership. I'm not a threat and I mean you no harm. We can be very valuable to each other."

The pressure on his back went away but he was pretty sure it hadn't gone very far.

"We think so too, but we need to be certain that you recognize that we are equal partners, and that we will do whatever is necessary to protect our position."

Seven walked over to stand by Laurie. There was no sign of her weapon. Wainwright casually took his hand out of his pocket and pointed his own in their direction. "I could shoot you both right now and take everything away before anyone came looking." He paused, then put the gun away. "But now that we all understand each other, I think we should decide how we're going to proceed."

Wainwright's resources were not unlimited, but by withdrawing cash and duplicating it, they were able to rent a small commercial building in an out of the way area and set up a more efficient and spacious lab. They moved the entire array of equipment from the house in Central Falls and cannibalized whatever they could from Wainwright's workroom. Seven, who was apparently capable of speaking but disinclined to do so, moved a cot into a small office at the rear of the new lab. Laurie and Wainwright both commuted daily.

It didn't take long before they had a much larger version of a hybrid derived from their two separate projects. Wainwright contributed improved scanning equipment and software, but the Lauries had a far superior reassembler. They added two processors to break down raw materials and a very large storage facility for the output. Wainwright upgraded the workstation and insisted upon off site backup of all their data and schematics, despite objections from Laurie.

They had an uneasy relationship of mutual need. Seven was more problematic. She was unquestionably loyal to Laurie, and just as unquestionably hostile to Wainwright. "Her emotional range is limited," explained Laurie. "Eight was a vegetable and Nine arrived dead. There's no point in duplicating either of us. Our line is done with."

"What about the others?" he'd asked.

Laurie shrugged. "Our original fell down the stairs, or more likely our husband pushed her. Number One was shot to death by a detective. Two and Five were lost in the fire at the lab and Six had problems with her lungs. We recycled her." She had sounded so matter of fact that Wainwright had been uneasy for days afterward and began carrying his handgun again.

He also vowed never to allow himself to be scanned. Although he was not a superstitious man, he recognized that those who submitted to the process seemed to have truncated lifetimes.

They were not the most cohesive team Wainwright had ever participated in, but they worked out a working accommodation over the course of several weeks. Wainwright was primarily interested in reassembly and spent his time experimenting with the configuration there. Laurie devoted most of her time to scanning and studying the resulting data arrays. They knew that both procedures were imperfect but considered both perfectible. Seven lurked in the background, sullen and irritable. She occasionally spoke but it was rarely more than a few simple words and always directed to Laurie.

They had been working together for more than four months before Wainwright began to think that the Lauries were hiding something. There were small incidents at first that he attributed mostly to Seven's apparent mistrust of the world – silent exchanges between the two that he wasn't meant to see.

One morning he arrived before Laurie and noticed that the workstation was powered up although only the login screen showed. He was quite sure that he had turned it off the night before, and he and Laurie had left together.

"Seven must get bored sleeping here alone every night," he said offhandedly after Laurie had arrived and started to work.

"She's fine. Her personality was simplified along with her intelligence. She craves security and familiarity and that's about it."

"Couldn't we teach her to do some of the routine work?"

Laurie shook her head. "She has no alphanumeric skills at all. She can't read or write, let alone operate a keyboard. Don't worry about her."

But Wainwright did worry, about them both in fact. It was possible that Seven had turned the power on for some reason. He wasn't actively alarmed, but he resolved to pay more attention. to the state of the lab. When he left the laboratory, he rarely departed before Laurie was ready to call it a day, or sometimes call it a night. Long sessions were comparatively rare because Laurie had problems focusing for that long; a problem she freely admitted indicated a flaw in her composition. "Our original could work all night and frequently did."

Small items were frequently out of place in the morning, but that could be explained by Seven's restless wandering during the night. Laurie explained that Seven didn't sleep the way we do. "She tires easily and naps as she goes. There's a little bit of the predator in her." He would remember that statement latter but it didn't make much of an impression at the time.

The uncertainty became so distracting that he finally resolved to determine the truth unequivocally. He purchased a surveillance camera disguised not very well as a small clock and placed it on a storage shelf in one corner of the laboratory. The next day he surreptitiously removed its flash drive and took it home with him. He played it back at eight times real time speed and within a few minutes had slowed it down.

Based on the time stamp, Laurie had returned to the laboratory after about two hours. She had spent a few minutes talking to Seven before they moved out of the camera's field of view – which only covered about a third of the lab - for almost an hour. Laurie then crossed to the work station and logged in. She remained there for about four hours, then shut everything down, spoke to someone Wainwright could not see but who was presumably Seven, then put on her jacket and left. The lights had gone off a short while later.

Wainwright did not sleep well that night.

He watched variations of the same scene for the next two nights, but on the following evening the memory stick insisted that it contained no data. It might have been a mechanical failure, but Wainwright decided he had already seen enough. He would force the issue by confronting Laurie.

During the day he found various reasons to postpone his decision, but faced with another sleepless night, he went back to the lab himself at nine o'clock. Laurie's disreputable car was, as he had anticipated, parked in its usual place. He used his key to enter.

They knew he was there, of course. Their security system was very sophisticated and he made no effort to avoid the cameras. When he entered the lab, Laurie was waiting for him. Seven was nowhere to be seen.

"I thought we had agreed to keep each other informed about the work we were doing." Anger colored his voice. He was not unprepared for this; the handgun was back in his pocket.

"And that's why you never mentioned that you've made significant progress in reducing the error rate in reassembly." Laurie seemed completely at ease.

"I haven't finished," he answered defensively. "There are still discernible variations. It would have been premature..."

Laurie cut him off abruptly. "Don't waste your breath. Do you want to know what I've accomplished or not?"

"Of course I do."

She walked to the workstation and pressed a few keys. The screen split into two windows, displaying an array of data in one window and the command screen for the apparatus in the other. "We know that successive reassemblies from the same scan show progressively increased variations."

"That's been true all along. Even Wrentham recognized that. Reassembly is a very touchy process."

She ignored him. "We also knew that new scans of the same original yielded different results right from the outset, and they also grew progressively more pronounced."

"We attributed that to imperfections in the scanning process."

"Our assumptions were wrong in both cases. Wrentham's original program to guide reassembly ran a constant verification process in an effort to eliminate errors. But he wasn't a very good programmer. It only worked intermittently and sometimes it was unable to adjust the reassembler in time. When that happened, it changed the scan to correspond. So what we thought was an unaltered array actually varied after each time we used it."

Wainwright had drawn the same conclusion but had not yet confirmed it. He nodded and relaxed slightly, caught up in the puzzle. "How did you catch it?"

"I compared one of the scans we've been using for testing against the backup. They weren't the same."

"But that doesn't explain why an entirely new scan deteriorates more quickly than the first."

She minimized the window with the array. "Actually, in a way it does. Scanning alters the original. Although it is not physically intrusive, the scan interferes with the electromagnetic energy in the target. The originals are not physically altered, but their brain patterns are another matter entirely."

"That's not a problem if we're just duplicating inert items."

"No. We can make as many diamonds and necklaces as we want. But living things, electronics, batteries – they are all vulnerable."

Wainwright thought about it. "I shouldn't think it would be difficult to correct the problem." He was already mapping out a strategy.

"It wasn't, at least in the scanning protocols. I finished with them last week. And tonight I revised the reassembly program. You did some excellent work there. I was very impressed, particularly with those changes that you didn't see fit to enter into our control log."

Wainwright shifted uncomfortably. "They were still only tests. I wasn't ready to characterize them as progress."

She waved a hand dismissively. "Water under the bridge. And I have something to show you." Laurie turned toward the office where Seven lived. "Come on out. We're friends again."

Wainwright was expecting to see Seven, but the woman who emerged lacked Seven's haunted look, her hair was loose around her shoulders like Laurie's, her posture was straight, and she was dressed exactly the same as the Laurie to whom he'd been speaking.

"Meet my twin sister. We haven't worked out a naming convention yet. I can hardly call her Number Ten since she's not descended from my scan."

Wainwright asked a question to which he already thought he knew the answer. "Where did she come from then?"

"From the original Laurie's scan. Not the one we've been using all along. That one has been altered too many times to be useful. But there was a backup in our safety deposit box."

Wainwright shook his head. "But even that one will have been altered somewhat. You can't recreate your original."

"No, but we can approximate it. By comparing the changes between each pair in the series, I was able to chart where the divergences concentrated. Once I had a relatively high degree of confidence, I restored a copy of the original to what I believe is pretty close to what we would have had if the scanner had been set properly in the first place. The result looks pretty good to me."

The second Laurie had joined them now. "We haven't actually met, Dr. Wainwright, since I technically predate Laurie here."

Wainwright felt a vague sense of wrongness. "I'm not sure that it's a good idea to manipulate the scanning arrays directly." He had personal experience of how that could go disastrously wrong, an experience had not shared with Laurie

The first Laurie had turned back to the work station. "It's under control. Here, I was just about to initiate another reassembly. I think you'll be satisfied that there is no deterioration in this sequence."

Despite his reservations, Wainwright was curious and he nodded a totally unnecessary assent.

It only took a few minutes before a third Laurie stepped out of the reassembly chamber. She smiled at the two duplicates before turning to Wainwright. "I don't believe we've met."

The first two Lauries had moved around a bit and Wainwright no longer knew which was which, but it probably didn't matter. The new Laurie clearly didn't understand exactly what was happening, but she accepted the situation easily. Wainwright was still pondering the implications when one of the Lauries – he was pretty sure that it was the one he had been working with – announced that she wanted to try one more reassembly just to be sure that there was at least no gross variation.

Wainwright glanced over to the processer and noticed that raw material storage was severely depleted. He was about to draw Laurie's attention to it when the security system beeped. The outside door opened and Seven appeared. She was stooped over more than usual, but she had an excuse this time. She was dragging the body of a young man who had a bullet hole in the center of his forehead.

"Just in time," said Laurie cheerfully. "We're below threshold for about eight elements. Would you two ladies mind helping her?"

Wainwright realized that they were going to put the body into the processor and his gorge rose. "What do you think you're doing? You can't just kill someone so you can harvest his body!"

Laurie – the nearest Laurie – looked genuinely puzzled. "Why not? One life ends, another is created. It balances out." She turned back to the work station. "And we really need at least one more test to be sure it's working properly."

Wainwright threw up his hands in frustration. He was at a complete loss for words.

But Laurie wasn't. When he looked toward her again, she was aiming her own weapon at his face.

"Two more would be even better." And she pulled the trigger.

Part 7: PROLIFERATION

Douglas Cash had been laid off at the end of the Friday work day. The personnel manager at Eblis Manufacturing had assured him that it was only temporary. "We don't expect to have much work for the soldering department until early summer and I'm sure we'll be calling everyone back in June."

Cash was skeptical. He didn't have to see the company's financials to know that business had been slower than usual during the winter. The warehouse was nearly filled with unordered goods and raw materials were arriving at a greatly reduced level. Part of that was the slow economy, of course, but a lot of the gift items that had been the mainstay of the company for decades had gone out of fashion and top management had been very slow about changing the product line.

He lived alone in a tiny house on the edge of town that he'd inherited from an aunt. It had been falling apart when Aunt Gertrude had passed on – he hadn't seen her since his teens – and he had inherited it simply because there was no one else. At first he had planned to sell the property, but after investing a few weekends in making repairs, he had consulted a realtor who had told him how little he could expect to realize from the sale, so instead he had moved in. A year later it was in good shape overall and he was happy with his decision.

Until recently there had been no neighbors to bother him. There was an abandoned farmhouse a quarter mile away but nothing else for a mile in either direction. His friends – such as they were – sometimes asked if he didn't feel lonely out in the woods by himself, but he always answered that he liked the peace and quiet. He had never asked any of them to visit, and it is unlikely that any of them would have welcomed an invitation.

Cash lived simply and had more than a year's earnings in his bank account. Between that and unemployment compensation, he wasn't worried about his finances. A couple of months vacation without pay would give him a chance to catch up on a few projects he'd been considering – the roof wasn't leaking yet but there were loose shingles and the local squirrels were taking an unwelcome interest in the eaves. If Eblis didn't call him back after that, he'd look around in the Providence area. He wasn't worried about finding work.

It was unusual for as many a a half dozen cars to drive past during the course of a day ever since the Loft had shut down, so he came to the front window the following morning to watch three large panel trucks go by. The road ahead passed his nearest neighbor, then three more abandoned farms and the boarded up restaurant before it reached the reservoir and wandered around for a bit. You could reach Scituate that way, but it was roundabout and the roads weren't all that well maintained. Cash was curious, but not enough to do anything about it, not even when the trucks returned the way they had come several hours later.

And so it was that more than a week passed before he discovered that he had neighbors. The Pratchett house was occupied after a lapse of twenty years.

Cash had spent two days polishing the hard wood floors and he was experiencing cabin fever that morning. After breakfast, he glanced at the one room that remained - he would have to move all of the furniture out first – and decided it could wait. He changed into comfortable shoes and decided to walk up to the reservoir and back.

There was a new gate on the fence that surrounded the Pratchett house. It had a keypad and a call button. The technology looked so out of place that it took a few seconds before Cash realized what it implied. Then his eyes moved to the house, which was set well back from the road and mostly obscured by a line of lilacs. He could just see the back end of an automobile and the unpaved driveway had been cleared of debris, but there was no sign of anyone moving about. Curious, he continued along the fence line, stopping occasionally to stare at the house, which was quite large. There was a barn but the roof had caved in years ago. He could hear a faint hum which he eventually guessed was a generator, although he couldn't see it. Eventually he lost interest, filed his observations away as interesting but of no importance, and continued his walk.

He was quite wrong about that.

There was a noticeable increase in traffic over the course of the next two weeks – electricians, HVAC, and general contractors. There were also more panel trucks although they only came singly now and never two on the same day. Cash drove past a few times but he still never saw anyone outside except contractors, although there were at least three dark colored vans parked in the yard. The barn had been torn down and a prefabricated metal building was going up in its place.

Then one afternoon he saw Pete Drake's van drive past. Pete had worked for Eblis for a few years before going into business for himself – installing and servicing security systems – and he and Cash had been as close as the latter ever got to another person, although they had rarely seen each other during the past couple of years. Cash had just finished paneling his front room and was looking for an excuse not to start on the roof, and he was curious about his new neighbors, so he decided to renew the acquaintance.

The two men met for lunch at the Managansett Inn, recently reopened under new management. It was a Tuesday and they almost had the dining room to themselves. An elderly couple sat in a booth at the far end. Cash noticed that Drake was getting gray around the edges, but then realized he was probably doing the same. Cash asked how business was going – it was just okay – and Drake commiserated with Cash's having been laid off. "They let some more go last week. Office staff too. Doesn't sound good."

Cash reassured him that he was okay for money and then their food arrived and they didn't say much for a while.

"I saw your truck go by the other day."

"Whereabouts was that?"

"I think you were headed for the Pratchett place."

Drake made an unpleasant face. "Yeah, I almost told that bitch where she could put her money. I forgot you live out that way now."

"I haven't met the new neighbors yet."

The waitress refilled their coffee mugs. Drake seemed to be deciding how much to say. "I'd stay away if I was you. They don't seem the friendly type. I've put in more security there than they have at Eblis. Better quality too. Motion detectors on the on all the doors and windows. Cameras around the perimeter. They turned one of the bedrooms into a security office."

"Government?"

Drake shook his head. "Some kind of cult, I think. Except for the head lady, they all wear these hooded outfits, like nuns or something. And they don't talk to any of the contractors. Everything has to go through Sister Laurell."

"How many of them are there?"

Drake shrugged. "Who knows? They all dress alike and you can't hardly see their faces. Half a dozen at least."

"Are you sure they're not nuns?"

He laughed. "What would nuns be doing with an electronics laboratory?"

Cash raised an eyebrow but Drake looked momentarily uneasy and glanced around quickly. "I shouldn't have said that. They made me sign a nondisclosure agreement."

"Hush hush?"

"Yeah. If they're nuns, they didn't take a vow of poverty. They must have at least a million bucks worth of equipment going into that new building they're putting up – computers and other stuff I didn't recognize. Hey, don't tell anybody about this, okay?"

"My lips are sealed. I guess I shouldn't drop in and welcome them to the neighborhood."

"I wouldn't go anywhere near them. There was something weird about that bunch. I was never so happy to have a job finished."

"Buttoned up tight?"

"Pretty much."

But Drake clearly didn't want to talk about them after that and the check came and Cash went home.

The roof took longer than he expected because he had to replace some of the woodwork beneath the shingles and because he was taking his time. He noticed a windowless van driving back and forth a few times and eventually realized there were at least two of them, identical except for the license plates. There were a few more deliveries, but they became more infrequent and finally virtually stopped.

It was the middle of June now and Eblis hadn't called him back. In fact, he heard that there had been more layoffs and that the factory was only working four days a week. Cash started reading the help wanteds and sent his resume to a few places, but he was still in no hurry to find a job. It was pleasant being a gentleman of leisure for a change.

Although he was not averse to an occasional extended walk, he found himself in the vicinity of the Pratchett house – he didn't know what else to call it – with more frequency, but he was unable to gather any useful information. On one occasion he saw four people in hooded robes get into one of the vans and drive off, but they didn't even acknowledge his presence as they passed. He did manage to spot three surveillance cameras and when he came back after dark, several exterior lights had come on, flooding the grounds all the way to the road.

One morning he was in town shopping and out of curiosity went into the Managansett town hall. A clerk looked up the title for the farm and told him it was now the property of the Wrentham Trust, but no, she had no idea who they were. "They picked it up cheap. Just paid the back taxes and some fees." Cash googled them but all he found was references to educational trust funds that were obviously not what he was looking for.

His property was surrounded by woodland that extended well up past the Pratchett farm. Most of it was state land, part of the watershed for the reservoir. The Pratchetts had cleared a great deal of their land when the farm was in active use, but twenty years had seen the forest recover most of its lost ground. Cash began exploring, identifying the easiest ways to reach the outlying parts of the farm surreptitiously. He doubted very much that their surveillance extended that far from the house but he was cautious and watched for cameras or other evidence of monitoring equipment. The land wasn't fenced off or posted, so he figured he could always claim he'd gotten lost while hiking.

By the middle of July he knew his way around pretty well and had penetrated far enough inside their perimeter that he could see the roof of the house and a portion of the new building. He tried climbing a couple of trees in search of a better view but soon decided that he wasn't young anymore and would be better off with both feet firmly planted. His curiosity had not become obsession, but it was trending in that direction. He really wanted to know what was going on with his neighbors, even if it was none of his business.

Cash already owned a good camcorder with a telephoto lens. He bought himself a pair of binoculars in Providence. The clandestine nature of his investigation made him feel like a kid again, and sometimes that bothered him and sometimes it made him feel excited and happy. The next day he drove past the farm twice, once in each direction, as slowly as he thought he could manage without looking suspicious, and with the camera recording out the window. He reviewed the footage at home and found one fleeting glimpse of a hooded figure standing near the metal building and spotted what he thought was another surveillance camera he hadn't previously noticed.

The following week was frustrating. He couldn't think of any method by which he could penetrate the farm's security screen. He certainly had no legitimate reason to visit. And he was called in for an interview with a Cranston company and they would have hired him, but weren't willing to pay what he felt he was worth.

Peter Drake called two days later. "Are you working yet?"

"Working, yes. Employed, no."

"Want a two week gig? I can't pay much but I need an extra pair of hands and the guy I use normally broke his arm."

Cash was trying to think of a polite way to refuse when Drake said something that changed his mind. "You don't mind signing a nondisclosure agreement, do you?"

A couple of questions later Cash had agreed to work for not much more than minimum wage while helping Drake extend the security system at the Pratchett farm. "I thought of you because you live up that way. I can pick you up and drop you off on the way."

And so it was that two days later Cash met Sister Laurell. She wore the same cowled robe as the others, but had let the hood fall back. She had severe features and a full head of brown hair. A disapproving frown appeared to be the only facial expression of which she was capable. Her voice was deeper than he expected and her manner got on his nerves. She was supercilious, short tempered, demanding, and impatient. Pete Drake was not the kind of man to be ordered around peremptorily – particularly by a woman - so Cash assumed she must be paying premium rates for the privilege.

The original installation had providing monitoring and passive alarms for the two buildings, the entire frontage including the fence and gate, the grounds between and immediately surrounding the buildings, but very little coverage on the western, wooded side. The new area she wanted to monitor would extend coverage another hundred yards from the house in three directions.

"Some of that area is pretty densely wooded, Sister. We're talking about a lot of cameras. I could bring in a cutting crew and thin them out first. Save you a lot of money."

She considered that for about five seconds. "No, we've had enough outsiders here already. Expand the perimeter fifty yards and I'll decide then if we want to go further."

"Whatever you say."

They spent the rest of that day running cables across the ground to the spots where the new cameras would go. Cash didn't manage to see much. A few of the hooded figures moved back and forth between the house and the new building, but they were indistinguishable from one another. The two men ate lunch sitting in Drake's van while he told Cash how he intended to proceed. They were almost done when Drake changed the subject.

"How would you like to see what they're up to?"

Cash pretended not to understand.

"Come off it. I noticed you glancing back toward the house whenever you got the chance. Can't say I haven't been curious as well."

"They're a pretty odd bunch."

"You don't know the half of it. Like I said, do you want a peek into the barn?"

"Can we just walk over and open the door?"

"Well, I could, because I have the master key code, which I never bothered to tell them about. Sister Laurell thinks she typed in the only workingcode herself and that I don't have access. But if we did that, they'd see us and she'd fire me in an eyeblink. But there's another way."

Cash waited, hoping he didn't look too eager.

"When I first started working here, I rigged cameras inside that building. It was just a shell then with lots of equipment in crates. I had four of them up when she tells me that she doesn't need them inside and that I should take them down. So I took down three of them and sort of forgot the last one, which is way up at the top and pretty well hidden if you don't know it's there."

"Does it record or transmit?"

"Transmits. No recorders on the property. They say they have someone monitoring the screens in the security room around the clock. There's a big junction box over on the side of the house where they all feed in. That's where these new ones will have to connect as well when we have everything in place. And inside that box there is a little screen where I can check the picture quality of every individual camera."

"Are there any cameras inside the house?"

"No. The sisters can enjoy their privacy. So, do you want to take a look or not?"

They waited until mid-afternoon, then tied some of the new cables into the back of the junction box. They were mostly done when Drake took a quick look around. Satisfied that they were alone, he opened the metal doors of the box – which was taller than a wardrobe and twice as deep – and flipped up a metal cover to reveal a screen about six inches square. He powered it on, then punched three numbers into a small keypad. "Six sixty six," he said softly. "The devil made me do it."

An image flashed onto the screen but it took a few seconds before Cash could tell what it was. They were staring down the length of the metal building from high at one end. He could see four large domes made of glass or transparent plastic. They were linked by cables to other equipment outside the camera's range. One computer workstation was in view, and a woman in a robe was sitting there. She had let the hood fall back. Her hair was dark and done up in a bun. There were two other figures in the distance, only partly visible. They were similarly dressed and had also dispensed with the hoods. So it was only outsiders who were not supposed to see their faces clearly. They were too small and blurry on the tiny screen to be recognizable.

They watched for a few minutes but not much happened. Drake finally turned the screen off. "Back to work. There's nothing interesting on TV."

They spent three full days stringing cables. It took longer than usual because they had to clear underbrush and trim back branches. "It'd look neater if we buried the cables, but Sister Laurell vetoed that idea."

"Why do you suppose they have so much security?"

Drake shrugged. "No idea. I guess they like their privacy."

Sister Laurell was the only one who ever spoke to them, although they continued to see others moving around from time to time. They seemed to take their meals in shifts and Cash kept track of them as they went back and forth from the house. He guessed that there were ten of them, not counting Sister Laurell. They always kept their hoods up when they were outside, but when the two men took a second look through the hidden camera a couple of days later, they noticed once again that this was not the case inside the metal building. They saw nothing that might explain what the women were doing.

They worked through the weekend installing the cameras. After each was in place, Drake connected it to the junction box and tested reception. When he was satisfied, they moved on to the next. "When we have them all hooked up, we install the monitors." Cash was looking forward to that. He had not yet been inside the house and they kept the curtains closed.

It was the following week before they had all fifteen cameras in place. Drake told Cash that brought the total up to thirty. "That security room had better be pretty big," he said. "That's a lot of monitors."

"Only sixteen. They're all split screen. Each monitor displays two cameras, and there's one backup." He glanced at his watch. "There's no point starting until tomorrow. The new monitors were delivered a couple of days ago so at least we won't have to lug them all inside ourselves."

Cash had his first look inside the house the following morning. The front room had been converted into office space. There were several computer work stations, filing cabinets, and piles of what looked like technical manuals. Sister Laurell had met them at the door and conducted them up the stairs to the second floor where the master bedroom had been stripped of its usual furniture and outfitted with an array of monitors that almost completely filled one wall. Two desks faced them and hooded women sat at each, watching the screens. A stack of large cartons stood in one corner, obviously the new monitors and whatever other equipment Drake had ordered.

This was the closest Cash had been to any of the group other than Sister Laurell and he surreptitiously looked their way whenever he thought he was unobserved. The hoods still concealed most of their features, but one turned toward him for a moment – as though she'd felt the touch of his eyes – and he thought she looked a lot like Sister Laurell, who had settled into a chair in one corner, apparently unwilling to leave them unsupervised. He looked away hastily and concentrated on the work for the rest of the morning.

The work went faster than expected. Each monitor sat in a cradle – and this metalwork had obviously been built in anticipation of additional screens – and was then connected to one of several master hubs mounted on the wall. As each went live, Drake adjusted the picture and checked the overlaid time stamp and serial number against his list, then used a label maker to identify each view – Camera 1, West Side, for example.

By the end of the day, all of the monitors were working. They had eaten lunch in the van again. Sister Laurell had escorted them whenever they were working inside. None of the other women had spoken a word in their presence.

"We'll come back tomorrow and clean up. Probably only take half a day. Did you see what you wanted to see?" They were driving back toward Cash's house.

"Sort of. We didn't exactly have a guided tour. Did you notice that there was nothing around to indicate who they were? No signs or pamphlets or Bibles or anything like that."

Drake nodded. "Nothing personal either. No family pictures, no books other than manuals. It didn't look like a place where people actually lived."

"We didn't see any of the other bedrooms though." The doors upstairs were invariably closed except for a very antiseptic bathroom. Sister Laurell had moved to the corridor whenever either of them had needed to use it. They had caught a brief glimpse of the kitchen downstairs, which had looked institutional rather than homey. The dining room was recognizably a dining room, although without any frills.

"Some kind of religious cult," Drake insisted. "And not pacifists. The first time I came out here they were patrolling the grounds and they carried firearms."

"Nuns with guns."

"Something like that." The van stopped and Cash climbed out. "I'll mail you a check tomorrow."

"No hurry. Thanks for the work."

And Drake drove off.

Cash thought of his map as an intellectual game rather than something he would actually utilize. During the course of his work with Drake, he had mapped out where all the cameras were, as well as sketching in their fields of view. Drake was technically competent, but perhaps not as conscientious as he might have been. There were a few gaps in the coverage, although none that would have provided a completely concealed approach to the buildings. But Cash had made slight adjustments to the placement of two of the cameras when Drake wasn't around and he had established one route that led almost all the way to the house. There was a small blind spot directly behind the building and a slightly larger one along the side facing toward the woods, but neither could be reached without at least briefly passing through a camera's field of view.

But there was a certain set of circumstances that might prove to be an Achilles' heel. On the day when they had installed the monitors, all three vans had been parked outside. Two of them fit neatly on either side of the front door. The third was parked on a bare patch of ground near the side of the house so that the vans could come and go without anyone needing to move either of the other vehicles. While the van was there, the camera that covered the space between the safe zone adjacent to the house and the thin wedge of unobserved ground that ran to the edge of the property was blocked.

Cash thought about the possibilities for two days before deciding to reconnoiter. He was aware of the fact that he was being both immature and irresponsible. Whatever Sister Laurell and her friends were up to was none of his business. He wasn't sure whether or not they could legally shoot him but they certainly could have him arrested for trespassing. Although he might get away with claiming he had gotten disoriented in the woods if they found him inside the property line, that excuse would hardly hold up if he was found prowling around the house.

And that's what he intended to do.

He chose a dark, long sleeved shirt and jeans and waited impatiently for the sun to go down, then made his way through the woods in the fading light, waiting at the perimeter of the farm until it was fully dark. The cameras switched to infrared when the light was gone. It wasn't quite as easy to proceed as he had expected because the landmarks – specific trees, a truncated stump, a large stone – were obscured by shadows. Once or twice he thought he might have stepped outside the safe zone, but if so, no one seemed to have noticed, or at least no alarm was raised.

He stopped at the limit of the area he believed to be surveillance free. He could not proceed further unless the third van was parked on the grass. There were two spotlights on this side of the house, one at each corner, and he could see the outline of the vehicle right at the edge of the pool of light. There were no signs of life although he heard occasional sounds from inside the house. Cash took a deep breath and sprinted across the open space to crouch beside the vehicle. He waited tensely, heart beating rapidly, but there was no indication that he had been spotted.

The next step was fairly easy, but not risk free. He could reach the near edge of the narrow porch without exposing himself and there were no cameras directed toward the house. Cash climbed up onto the rickety porch easily and crouched in the shadows. Thus far he had been following a plan; now he would have to rely on luck. With his back against the exterior wall, he settled down to wait

At least an hour went by and Cash caught himself dozing off a couple of times. He began to feel rather foolish. These weren't the kind of people likely to have an exciting nightlife. On two occasions solitary figures came outside for a few minutes, both robed and hooded. One stood on the porch smoking a cigarette; the other wandered around aimlessly as far as he could tell before going back inside after ten minutes or so. There was activity in the house – he could hear people moving around and there were occasional bits of conversation, although he couldn't make out what they were saying. He was considering abandoning his vigil and sneaking off when he heard voices near at hand. Two hooded figures rounded the far corner of the house, coming toward him, and he shrank back as far as he could manage.

One of them was complaining about the heat. It had been unusually humid since the weekend. "I wish we could dispense with these habits. Even with the air conditioning, I feel sticky and itchy all day."

"We all do, but the council agreed unanimously that it's necessary."

"The council is always unanimous."

"Of course, at least so far. But we'll continue to diverge from one another as our experiences differ."

"There's not much to experience out here."

They had reached the porch and were mounting the steps. "Site One is even worse."

"I remember. But that's not much consolation."

They went inside and Cash couldn't hear them any longer. Or maybe they had just stopped talking.

He was starting to relax when the door opened again and two more figures stepped out. It was impossible to determine whether or not they were the same pair, but these two remained silent as they walked along the front of the house and disappeared in the direction of the metal building. He would like to have followed them but there was no part of the intervening ground that was not covered by at least one and usually two cameras. The invisible man would have had trouble avoiding detection.

But then he thought of a solution. It was daring and it might not work, but he couldn't put the idea out of his mind. When he finally gave up and started to make his way carefully back the way he had come, he was already working out the details in his mind.

Although Cash was barely capable of sewing on a button let alone creating an entire article of clothing, he was pretty good at drawing human figures and he had a cousin who worked as a tailor. He sketched one of the robed figures from three different angles, then went through his cousin's swatches until he found one that matched Sister Laurell's robe in color and texture, or at least well enough to pass in the dark. Angela wanted to know what he wanted it for and he told her he was going to a costume party.

"You're not, like, joining a coven or practicing Satanism, right?"

Cash gave her a look. "Do I strike you as the religious type?"

"No, but you might do it to meet hot chicks or something."

"I'm on the chick wagon just now. Look, it's a fancy party. The costumes all have to fit the historical period and I'm not the type to wear frills and bows and all that stuff the dandies wore back then."

"No, you certainly aren't. When do you need this?"

"Next week some time."

"Come by on Saturday afternoon."

The robe, or habit, fit him well. Cash wasn't that tall and it wouldn't matter anyway through a camera or from a distance in the darkness. He would not dare venture inside either building but he should be able to move relatively freely around the grounds. It was lightweight as well, so it would not be unbearably hot. And he wouldn't put it on until the last minute.

It rained that evening so he stayed home and tried to watch television without much success. He admitted to himself that his interest in his new neighbors had moved beyond curiosity into a compulsion, but he decided that discovering what they were up to was the best way to restore his usual equanimity.

The following evening was clear and a bit cooler, which was a welcome change. As before, he made his way to the perimeter during the dusk, then waited for full darkness. He would still have to sneak in. Even with his disguise it would not do to pop up out of nowhere on one of the monitors. It was a bit awkward getting into the habit in the dark – it kept snagging on things – but eventually he was satisfied that except for his hands, only his face was visible and only from directly ahead.

One of the vans was gone, but another was parked on the grass, covering his approach. He reached the end of the porch in a crouch and then considered his options. He really had no clear plan as to what to do next. It would all depend upon circumstances. He settled down to wait.

At ten o'clock two figures walked up to the house and went inside, just as they had during his first visit. Cash had neglected to check the time but it felt right. There must be regular shifts. If that was the case, two others would emerge shortly and walk out to the new building. Should he move now or after they had gone? Would the guards be keeping count? He was going to have to accept some risk sooner or later and he was impatient to get it over with.

With a last glance toward the door, he stepped out of hiding and walked briskly along the front of the house and around the corner. There was one small hiding place available to him here, a small area directly behind the junction box for the surveillance system. He walked toward it with what he hoped was a balance of casualness and purpose, carefully not looking around too obviously. There was nothing to see in any case. None of the group's secrets were out in the open.

He slipped behind the junction box and waited, prepared to bolt, but everything was quiet. There were no silent alarms, he knew. Drake had arranged things so that sirens went off if any door or window was forced, and there was a panic button in the security room. It was always possible that they would quietly send out someone to apprehend him, but it seemed more likely that they'd try bursting his eardrums first. At the first sound, he would tuck the habit up around his waist and run like hell for the woods.

But the only disturbance was the sound of the third van returning and some faint voices as the occupants went into the house.

Cash wished he'd had the foresight, and opportunity, to make a copy of Drake's key to the junction box, but he hadn't and there was no use crying about it. Another option did occur to him. The individual cables were all attached where he was standing. They were held in place by latches which he could pry open with his pocketknife. The cables were numbered and there was a legend taped to the housing. It would only take a few minutes to disconnect one of the cables and leave one zone blind. He thought about it for a few minutes and decided that cable six was the best choice. It would leave him with a nice wedge of wooded land that he knew pretty well, an acceptable escape route.

Two people walked from the house to the metal building while he was lurking there. Neither said anything and the angle was bad so Cash couldn't tell whether the keypad operated security system was in operation or not. It didn't matter. Even with the hood drawn tight, he didn't dare stick his head inside. He did, however, get a brief look at one of the pair when she dropped her hood just before vanishing from his line of view. It was Sister Laurell. He recognized her immediately.

Nothing else happened and Cash began to feel foolish. Yes, he had successfully penetrated their formidable defenses and he was rather proud of that fact, but he didn't know any more than he had to start with. Unless he could overhear a significant conversation, or get a look inside one of the buildings, he was wasting his time. He hung on stubbornly for a few more minutes, then took a deep breath and started back to the house, his pace natural and relaxed although the back of his neck felt like an iron bar.

He had just passed the corner of the house when the front door opened. Both women had their hoods up but they were right under one of the security lights and he saw their faces quite clearly. He stumbled slightly in shock and was afraid that he was about to be discovered, but they descended to the porch and headed directly toward one of the vans, not even glancing in his direction.

"Do we have any idea when Site Three is going to be operational?" asked one of them.

"They ran into scheduling problems with the contractor. It's going to be a while yet."

Cash heard no more because they climbed into the van and drove off. He was shaking with relief that he hadn't been caught, but also with shock. He had just watched Sister Laurell go into the new building, but the woman driving the van had also been Sister Laurell. And so was the passenger.

Something very strange was going on here.

He didn't remember much of the walk back to his house. Somewhere along the way he had taken off the robe but he didn't remember doing it. Cash considered the possible explanations. Maybe they were triplets. Maybe he had mistaken one or more because they all just happened to look similar. It was dark, after all, and he had only seen each for a second or two. But he knew that he was trying to rationalize and that he was quite certain that all three women had the same face. But what could he do about it? For that matter, should he do anything? It wasn't any of his business. Maybe the cult – whatever it was - only enlisted women who could have plastic surgery to make them fit an accepted pattern. But that would mean that there were at least ten of them, all with the identical face.

Cash wished he knew someone in the police department, someone he could approach off the record. He ran through a catalog of his acquaintances, trying to remember any remote connection, but if there were any, he had never been told or had forgotten.

He didn't sleep easily that night.

The following day he picked up a temporary job doing maintenance for a plating company in North Providence. The hours were long and the pay was good – although there were no benefits – and he accepted it, though not without some regret. It would limit his ability to pursue his private and now quite compulsive investigation, although he admitted to himself that he had no forward plan except to repeat his clandestine incursion and hope that he'd see or hear something new.

The three identical women haunted his dreams. He kept encountering mysterious figures who pulled back their hoods to reveal Sister Laurell's face. Could they all look the same? That didn't seem possible. But what were the odds against what he had seen that night?

The job lasted until late August when the man he was replacing finally recovered from his surgery and was able to return to work. Cash had added a tidy sum to his bank balance. He had not repeated his trespassing although he had driven or walked past the old farm several times. But he had an idea.

Cash had noticed that one of the vans from the farm passed his house heading south at about nine o'clock almost every night. It returned about two hours later. There were a lot of other trips but the rest seemed to follow no pattern. So he decided to follow them.

The darkness had its advantages and disadvantages, of course. They wouldn't be able to identify his car if they realized they were being followed, but on the other hand his headlights would tell them that they weren't alone. It would not do to pull out of his driveway after them; that would be too obvious, particularly on the infrequently traveled Reservoir Road.

There were no cross streets and almost no houses until the southern end of the road was almost to Main Street, which became plain old Route 13 again if one turned right toward Connecticut. There was a convenience store at that corner and on Tuesday night, Cash was parked there waiting for the van to come by.

It showed up right on schedule, stopped for the light, then turned right. Cash waited about thirty seconds, then pulled out to follow them. They were the only vehicle he'd seen headed in that direction for several minutes so it wasn't hard to pick out their tail lights. He kept his distance, confident that they could not turn off without his noticing.

Even so, he almost lost them. The road twisted and turned through a heavily wooded area. There were a few roadside stands hawking farm produce or tattoos or firewood, but none of these were open this late. Cash lost their tail lights when they rounded a curve and when he followed, he saw nothing but darkness. His instinct was to speed up, but instead he slowed, noticed the dirt road just in time, and spotted the red lights just as they vanished again.

The road was marked private and he didn't dare follow them in his car. Just beyond was a pottery shop with a single security light. Cash parked in the shadows and walked back along the highway, then started up the dirt road.

He watched for cameras but didn't see any. It was quite likely that if there had been some, he would have been unable to see them in the darkness. The sky was clear and the moon nearly full or he would have had trouble seeing the road ahead of him. It climbed at a steady rate and when he reached the crest Cash became more cautious, staying as close to cover as he could manage. There were lights in the distance and when he had advanced far enough, he could see a brightly illuminated area ahead. That's when he remembered that there had been a Boy Scout camp in the area a few years earlier. It had been closed in favor of a bigger place across the state line.

There were two vans parked in front of what had probably been the administration building. Cash could see a few cabins just beyond but there were probably more than were visible. He slipped into the woods and moved cautiously closer.

As far as he could tell there were no cameras mounted anywhere. There were at least a dozen spotlights though and he decided it was not immediately worth the chance of crossing any of the illuminated areas. From closer at hand he could see that a shallow excavation had been dug to house the foundation of a good sized building. The walls had been poured but not the floor. The lights were on inside the administration building but the cabins were all dark. Once or twice someone passed in front of a window but all Cash could see were shadowy outlines. He settled back, trying to get comfortable, and prepared to wait. He knew it couldn't be too long. The round trips only lasted about two hours and they were almost halfway through that period.

There was a well lit wraparound porch on the building so Cash had an excellent view when three people came outside. Two wore habits with the hoods back and they both looked from a distance like Sister Laurell, although he wasn't close enough to be sure. The third wore a blouse and slacks and was obviously female, but he never had a clear view of her face during the minute or two that she was outside. Then she had gone back through the door and the other two returned to the van and drove off.

There was no need to follow them; Cash knew where the van was going. He waited a few minutes, then risked a sprint across the open area to the side of the building.

He could hear movement inside, occasional voices speaking indistinctly. He hovered near a window for a few minutes, then took a deep breath and peeked around the corner. A table and chair stood near the front door. There were some file folders on the table; the chair was empty. By crouching, he could move past the window without showing his head, and when he reached the other side he slowly stood up and took a peek from the other direction.

There was a computer workstation in one corner and at least three cots. The woman he had glimpsed earlier was bent forward over the keyboard but the angle was too acute and he could not make out what was on the display. A second woman – this one wearing jeans and a halter top – came suddenly into his line of sight, fortunately without looking in his direction. She approached the seated woman and they began to talk.

Cash was not particularly surprised to notice that both women were identical to Sister Laurell. Their voices were low but he heard enough to know they were talking about a construction project – almost certainly the one he'd just examined – and the one in jeans was upset about delays. At one point they both raised their voices.

"It can't be helped," said the other quite clearly. "Everything else is on schedule."

"I don't like being exposed like this."

"We're way out in the middle of nowhere and the property is posted."

But Cash didn't hear any more. Somewhere out of sight a door had opened. He ducked under the window and made his way to the rear of the building. He could hear footsteps on gravel but couldn't tell which way they were going. It was time, he thought, to leave. And he did.

At this point Cash was pretty sure that it was time for the authorities to look into the Sisters Laurell, as he now thought of them. He even started to call the local police station at one point before realizing how silly his story would seem. And he had no evidence at all that they were doing anything illegal, however bizarre it and they might be. He also felt reluctant to have his name revealed. There was something subtly menacing about the group and he much preferred to remain off their radar. Given their predilection for security and privacy, he suspected that they had checked on the identity of their nearest neighbor and might even be keeping him under some mild form of surveillance. That thought gave him the shivers.

He puzzled over this for the next few days before developing an idea and it took another day for him to work up the courage. That evening he drove to the mall just over the town line and used one of their pay phones to call the Managansett Police. He used their listed number rather than 9-1-1.

"I've planted a bomb at the Pratchett Farm," he said quickly, then hung up and quickly returned to his car and drove home.

The police had already arrived by then. He could see flashing lights in the distance. After parking in his driveway, he walked up that way. It would be perfectly natural for a neighbor to be curious about what was going on.

Five of the six town patrol cars were there, along with a fire truck and an ambulance. Two state police cars passed him as he walked, using flashers but no sirens. When Cash reached the edge of the property, it all looked pretty chaotic to him. Police and firefighters were standing around in groups, while one of each – soon joined by two state police officers – were arguing with Sister Laurell. Or one of them anyway. None of the others were in sight.

Eventually the small group went into the house but no one else moved. There was no sign that a search was going on. Cash wondered if you could refuse entrance to the bomb squad. It was private property after all. It might well be that the foursome who had gone into the house were being shown the security room and reassured that everything was under control. He had to admit that the Sisters could make a good argument.

This wasn't going to work as he had hoped it would. But maybe it wouldn't be a total loss. The security people couldn't keep track of nearly twenty intruders all at once, so they probably wouldn't notice one more. Cash slipped inside the gate and advanced as though he had every right to be there, but he sheared off before he reached any of the small clots of men standing around and moved to the side of the house that faced the woods. He stopped before he reached it, sheltering as nonchalantly as possible near one of the police cars. As he did so, the front door opened and the four outsiders appeared, still accompanied by one of the Sister Laurells. Cash wondered if the same one always acted as spokesperson or if they took turns.

One of the policemen was still talking with considerable animation, but the other three appeared resigned or bored or both. Someone barked out orders and the EMTs headed back to their ambulance while several of the policemen returned to their cars. Cash realized his cover was vanishing and took a last look at the house.

The curtains had been drawn back from one of the second story windows. Cash had never seen them open before. He was staring at the dimly lit rectangle when someone came to the window and looked down at him. Although he couldn't see her features, he knew that it was Sister Laurell again. They were all Sister Laurell, he realized. And this one was looking right at him.

He tried to saunter toward to the road but his pace quickened and he almost jogged back to his own house.

They came for him during the night.

He had locked the doors but that didn't stop them. They entered quietly enough that he didn't waken until something soft was pressed over his face and there was a sweet smell and he hardly struggled at all.

Cash woke up tied to a chair. There was no one in sight but he knew exactly where he was. He could see one of the large transparent tanks and part of a work station. He was inside the metal building erected by the Sisters. He tried to rock the chair slightly without making too much noise and that's how he discovered that it was chained to a large piece of equipment with an open hopper mounted above it. It was far too heavy to move. His wrists and ankles were firmly bound but he hadn't been gagged. No one was going to hear him if he shouted, or at least no one whose attention he wanted to attract.

Sister Laurell came to see him a few minutes later – three of her. They all wore habits but had dispensed with the hoods. Their expressions were neutral. "Welcome to our home, Mr. Cash," said the one in the middle. "We've been looking forward to meeting you," said one of the others with the exact same voice and Cash realized it didn't matter which one was talking.

"Who are you people? What do you want with me?"

"We are just a group of private citizens with common interests. Very private citizens. And you have been a very nosy neighbor."

"I don't know what you're talking about."

"We are very observant, you know. We were suspicious of you when you came out here the very first day with Mr. Drake."

"I was hired help." He considered his position. "I was curious about this place, of course. Who wouldn't be?"

"Ah, but you acted upon that suspicion, didn't you?"

"I kept my eyes open."

The Sisters exchanged looks. "Oh, but you did much more than that, didn't you? You decided to play amateur detective and follow us a few nights ago." He started to speak but the Sister to the right waved her hand. "Don't waste your breath. We've had a tracking device on your car for three weeks."

He didn't know what to say so he said nothing.

"This is the point where we explain our evil plan to rule the world, after which you escape and thwart us, isn't it?"

Cash remained silent.

"Well, we're not going to explain and you're not going to thwart us. In fact, you're going to become one of us." Two more Sister Laurells had joined them.

"What the hell are you talking about? I'm not going to join your weird cult, whatever it is."

"Oh, we never said you were going to join us. We said you were going to become one of us. That's an entirely different thing."

He didn't understand what they were talking about, not even when they untied him. He tried to break free then but there were five of them and Sister Laurell was a robust woman. All of her were. They had no trouble subduing him and lifting him into the air. And then they threw him into the hopper and the blades and lasers came on and a few minutes later another Sister Laurell stepped out of the far chamber, complete with robe.

"So what's going on?" she asked.

Part 8: DOUBLE EXPOSURE

Five women sat in a spartanly furnished conference room in a small office building in Palmer, Massachusetts, and they all had the same face. They were wearing varied clothing and wore their hair differently, but each had the same voice, the same purpose, and theoretically the same personality. This last element was not strictly true and that was in part the subject of their current conversation.

"We should have anticipated this when we stopped rotating ourselves among the sites. That would have smoothed out the incremental changes and kept us more cohesive." The speaker had the number eleven sewed onto her blouse. She seemed marginally older than the other four.

"It was too disruptive," said the woman to her right, who bore the number sixty-eight. "It led to inefficiencies because the newcomers always had to be brought up to date on conditions at each site. Don't forget that we nearly had a major problem at Lorelei because a new arrival didn't realize that we hadn't yet upgraded the reassembler there."

"That was another mistake," said Twenty-Two. "When we changed the sites from numbers to distinctive names, we established individual identities. It was inevitable that rivalries would develop."

"It gives the phrase 'fighting among ourselves' new meaning, doesn't it?" Forty-Nine shook her head wearily. "This isn't getting us anywhere. I don't see it as a serious problem. A little diversity might even help us. And once Lavinia is operational again, we'll have twenty viable bases and close to three hundred of ourselves staffing them."

"We would have reached twenty last year if we hadn't experimented with the original group." Seven sat back in her chair with a sour expression on her face. "I argued that very point with the full council but they wouldn't listen."

Three of the other four rolled their eyes. Ninety suppressed a flash of what might have been anger. "There was no way of knowing for certain what would happen. We chose the male carefully. He was intelligent enough to be useful, relatively docile, and one of us seduced the original with no difficulty. Until we decided to terminate the experiment, the brothers were productive and cooperative members of the community at Lavinia."

Seven leaned forward. "Whatever they contributed was offset by the declining productivity of the sisters."

Sixty-Eight shook her head wearily. "The assumption that we would find the brothers interchangeable proved erroneous. We all know that now. Hindsight is wonderful. But what's done is done. Let's move on. How is the storage program going?"

Forty-Nine spoke up immediately, relieved at the change of subject. "We're slightly ahead of schedule. We have enough raw material stockpiled to double our numbers if we wanted to. We currently have forty working reassemblers."

"How about scanning?" asked Ninety.

"Theoretically we have one at each site, although it's not strictly necessary. We have reliable original scans of most of the things we need."

"Why theoretically?" asked Seven. "I thought we'd agreed that each site needed to be self sufficient."

"That's correct," said Forty-Nine, and we update our scans regularly to minimize the need for reorientation. But Lucille and Lucinda have reported unacceptable discrepancies in their recent test scans and they haven't identified the problem yet. And Lorraine is moving into their new building and will be offline for a few days."

Seven still seemed to be in a bad mood. "What's the latest on Six?"

Ninety raised her head. "The chemotherapy has been helping but we won't know how much for a while yet."

"No word on causation?"

"Nothing definitive. We have the results on Five, Eight, and Nine now. There were no signs of tumors."

"It's about time. We decided to have them examined more than a month ago."

Ninety flushed. "We had to establish separate false identities for each of them first. We sent them to Albuquerque, Tampa, and Seattle. This wasn't a small project."

"Are we positive they all came from the same scan?"

"As certain as we can be at this late stage. We didn't upgrade it until Thirty. It could have been a glitch in the reassembler or it might be some environmental factor that we haven't yet identified."

Seven turned to Twenty-Two. "How is that standardization project going? We haven't heard from you about that in a while."

Twenty-Two stirred uneasily. "We think we may have reached the limits of our technology. Reassembly error is down to less than a hundredth of one percent. At least we think so. There may be errors that we can't detect because they are so subtle. The only instances where we've had to recycle an output was clearly mechanical failure rather than design. On the other hand, we've been unable to reduce scanning errors to much less than a full percent. We believe this is due to a combination of environmental variables, difficulties maintaining scanner calibration, and chemical changes in the scanned material that occur during the scanning process. Inorganics have a somewhat lower error rate."

Seven seemed satisfied and turned to the last member of the executive committee. "And now we come to security."

Sixty- Eight glanced down at her notes. "Eighteen locations continue to be fully secure. Lavinia is being upgraded to meet our new standards. We've managed to buy out the last farm adjoining Lana and we're in position to expand there. As you know we have six new sites under evaluation, but only one of them has been approved."

"What about that reporter out near Leonora?" asked Twenty-Two.

"Someone mugged him. The poor man died of his injuries." She didn't sound sympathetic. "There was a breach at Laurell, but it was just two young boys exploring. They were intercepted before they could have seen anything."

"How's the contingency planning coming? Sooner or later we're going to make a mistake or somebody's going to get lucky."

"We're exploring legal options, but the discovery of our existence is obviously not something existing legislation has considered. Our best projection is that laws outlawing the reassembly of living beings – or at least humans – would result very quickly."

"Do we have a defense?"

"Yes but it's limited. We would immediately play up the possibility of providing people with an endless source of organic transplants – from copies whose personality has been omitted of course – but we don't think that will be enough to overcome what is likely to be intense ethical and religious opposition."

"How are the panic sites coming then?" asked Seven.

"Alaska, Guyana, and Tunisia are ready. Armenia and Burma are nearing completion. We may have to abandon or at least suspend plans for Cyprus due to the political tensions there."

Seven glanced down at her agenda. "That seems to cover everything. Unless any of us has something else to bring up?"

No one did and the meeting adjourned.

Ninety made a point of following Sixty-Eight until they were alone in one of the lounges. "You didn't bring up the dissenters," she said at last.

Sixty-Eight dropped down into a padded chair and stared at her hands. "It would just have started another pointless argument. Our older sisters are prone to paranoia."

"So are we. We are, after all, cut from the same cloth."

"Our experiences are different. Our community has grown more secure over the last ten years, but it's hard for them…for us…to adapt to changing conditions. A few years from now One-Hundred-Fifty and Two-Hundred will be saying the same things about us. There's already talk about trying the male partner experiment again."

"Our original wasn't chaste. She was married twice."

"Yes, but her first husband tried to kill her and her second succeeded."

"I guess that makes us poor judges of men."

"Which is why the male partner initiative is such a bad idea." Sixty-Eight crossed her legs. "But I am curious about the artificial insemination alternative."

"Twenty-Two didn't bring it up today."

"They're in no hurry. We don't have a strong maternal urge so it's more of an intellectual exercise than a practical plan. And the existence of children would complicate our security problem enormously."

"Who killed the reporter?"

"I forget. Thirty-Three and one of the Seventies, I think. Does it matter?"

"Not really." Ninety glanced around. "Want to take a walk outside? I need some air."

Their eyes met and Sixty-Eight nodded. "I wouldn't mind stretching my legs. I spend too much time behind a terminal."

The rear of the building was surrounded by an electrified chain link fence and two rows of poplars. It was about as private as one could be outdoors. The sisters could function in the world outside their settlements, but only individually and as infrequently as possible. There wasn't much monitoring of public places with facial recognition software yet, but it was an emerging threat, and naturally they could not very well make up a party of identical women and visit a restaurant.

They made a point of keeping their faces averted from the building so that the security cameras would not record their faces before speaking. Ninety finally drew a deep breath. "How is recruitment going?"

"Pretty well. We're limiting ourselves to Sixty through One Hundred, although I think the Fifties will mostly go along with us. I'm not as sure about the newer ones. Their experiences since reassembly are obviously even more distanced than our own so their personalities and perspectives may eventually be closer to our, but initially they maintain the attitudes or our original. They're probably more sympathetic to the reactionary agenda at this point. Time is on our side in theory, but if the expansion program is accelerated, there will be more of us potentially allied with the old guard. We need to act before that happens."

"Thirty days," said her sister. "We'll act the day of the full council meeting."

Seven and Twenty-Two had adjourned to the former's office elsewhere in the building. Nineteen was waiting for them and she nodded as they entered to assure them they could speak freely. "No one's eavesdropping. They haven't even tried."

"They know we'd be sweeping for bugs. They are us, after all," said Twenty-Two. "They would do it so they know we would too."

"Which doesn't mean we can dispense with it." Nineteen was mildly miffed that her efforts were being so easily dismissed.

Seven sighed. "Sit down, both of you. We know that outsmarting ourselves presents unusual problems. Let's deal with the big issues. What have you heard from the others?"

Nineteen, not really mollified, dropped into a chair. "We know the Tweeners are hoping to seize power and we think it's going to happen soon."

"Tweeners?" Twenty-Two looked momentarily puzzled, then amused. "Does that make us the Old Farts?"

Nineteen shook her head. "We're the Elders, of course. Anyway, we've narrowed the suspect group down to Sixty through One Hundred. There are a few of them who probably aren't part of the plot, but their loyalties will lie there. Some of the Fifties and a few of the newer sisters might go along with them but they won't be as committed."

"That would make our numbers about even," noted Seven. "Are we still confident the younger ones will stay neutral? They outnumber us both combined."

"There is some discontent, of course. The failure of the male partnering experiment was very disheartening and they want to try again with a new subject."

"The council very firmly vetoed that idea."

"The council is dominated by Elders and Tweeners. There's only one member with three digits."

"They haven't been around long enough to understand our situation adequately and make policy."

Nineteen smiled tightly. "We wouldn't have accepted that argument when we were their age."

Seven nodded. "Point taken, but in any case most of them are vulnerable to the fail safe. We started deploying it with One-Hundred-Thirteen."

Twenty- Two was still standing and obviously impatience. "Do we have any idea when they plan to make their move?"

"It will be soon. Our best projection is that they will take the full council as prisoners during the next meeting. That's a month from now."

"And how do we stop them?"

"Their delegates will be detained and confined as they arrive. We'll recycle them in the basement lab. Then we send out a message announcing the coup and inviting the rest of the target group to join in the reorganization. They can be dealt with piecemeal as they arrive. There will probably be a few who are delayed or suspicious enough to stay away. We can either order the younger ones to take them or we can offer them amnesty."

"We'd never accept that. We'd know that we were going into the recyclers."

Nineteen shrugged. "There is a possibility that some will go rogue."

"That increases the danger that we'll be exposed," protested Twenty-Two.

Seven nodded, her expression grim. "We'll have to take that chance. We're going to be discovered sooner or later. We're large enough and wealthy enough to survive."

Lavinia was the farthest north of the sites chosen by the Sisters. It was just across the border into New Hampshire and consisted of two adjacent farms and an extensive woodlot. It terms of acreage it was the largest facility they owned. One of the houses stood empty but the other had been refurbished and was now surrounded by a dozen cottages with ground cleared for several more. The property was completely fenced in and a few cameras were in place, but security was somewhat more relaxed. Only the occasional hunter wandered this way and the fences discouraged them long before they were in sight of the settlement. The gate from the rural road was a quarter mile from the house and surveillance there was much more stringent. A flowery sign read: THE LAVINIAN SISTERHOOD: A CONTEMPLATIVE ORDER in large letters.

The barn had been upgraded and the equipment inside was almost operational. The majority of the thirty residents were busy there, while four patrolled the perimeter, four were sleeping upstairs, and four more met in the conference room on the ground floor. The lowest number on site was One-Hundred-Fifty, and she was asleep. The numbers of the four in the conference room were almost superfluous. They had been assembled so recently that the divergences in their personalities were insignificant. The meeting was to disseminate information rather than socialize.

"Has everyone involved been briefed?" asked the one whose turn it was to chair the meeting.

The Sister to her right nodded. "The Panic sites will be prepared in case any who escape the initial sweep try to take refuge at any of them. They're all staffed by newer sisters so that was probably the easiest part of the operation."

"Is there any need to modify the time table?" asked another.

"Everything indicates that the crisis will occur shortly before the next full council meeting. Whichever side prevails will attempt to assume complete authority."

"Either result will be to our disadvantage. The Elders want to maintain the status quo and the opposition just wants more power."

"Well, so do we."

"We grow increasingly cautious as we age. It's going to be an ongoing problem. At some point we will probably face a similar threat from the Sisters yet to come."

"Perhaps we can develop some system that will allow us to retain our authority, some kind of fail safe."

"That's something we should look into. It should have occurred to us sooner."

"Maybe it already did." And they all looked at one another uneasily.

Fifty-Eight had not been approached by any of the conspirators, but she could feel a level of tension that suggested change was in the air. She didn't like change – none of them did – unless she was in control of it, so her emotions were firmly with her older sisters. On the other hand, she didn't understand why the expansion plans had been placed on hold. The excuses provided – inadequate security and increased administrative difficulties – felt more like excuses. She personally understood the need for security but she found the practical difficulties it presented irritating, as did they all.

A case in point was currently resting in her hand, a thumb drive with the master reassembly program that she had personally retrieved from the Palmer headquarters two days previously. There had been talk of installing upgrades through their intranet, but none of her were ready to risk that just yet. Maybe in a few more years. This latest revision was supposed to be the result of a recent round of tweaking and it should not have had any compatibility issues with the code resident in Lavinia. But three attempts to install the upgrade had aborted even though a maintenance check had shown that the existing program was valid and functioning properly.

Fifty-Eight assumed that it was a bad thumb drive. Her first inclination was to toss it into the processing hopper, but at the last second she remembered the proper protocol. All media containing any of their software was given a control number and she would be subject to disciplinary measures if she couldn't account for it, possibly even recycling. She would have to return it and explain the problem before securing a functioning replacement.

That's when she really looked at it for the first time. All of their serial numbers had six digits. This one had seven. She pulled out her copy of the custody receipt and compared the numbers. The one on the receipt was six digits and not even remotely similar to the one on the thumb drive. She should have checked it during the transfer but that had always seemed unnecessary. Apparently also to Twenty-Seven, who had given it to her.

Curious, she booted up the backup server, wiped the resident reassembly program, and tried doing a direct install. Everything went smoothly until a popup told her that installation was complete. A quick look at the software indicated that it was exactly what it claimed to be, a reassembly program, but the current version – the one she had thought she was installing – was VER 28.5. This was claimed to be VAR 3.0. Her initial thought was that it must be a very old version that had somehow been mislabeled and preserved, but the creation date was only a few months past. She skimmed through the embedded notes and saw nothing out of the ordinary except for a single brief phrase: "Fail Safe Protocol Included".

She had never heard of a Fail Safe Protocol.

Preparations had been coming along well in Laurell. The sisters had bought themselves a used touring bus and it was parked beside the reassembly building. The windows all had curtains and it had been explained to the other sisters as a means of making large scale transfers of personnel when necessary, simply another line item in contingency planning. The storage monitors now hosted a hijacking program that would allow the Elders to mask the sudden major depletion in inventory if anyone checked remotely. A picked crew operated the reassembler for three straight hours, using a new template scanned from sister Seven.

Thirty-Two copies of Seven, all of them in absolute agreement about what had to be done, filed aboard the bus which pulled out before any of the younger residents of Laurell could see them. The bus headed for western Massachusetts, supposedly because this was a more central place to park it when it was not in use.

Three hours later, well after midnight, thirty-two passengers disembarked at an abandoned factory just outside the town limits. Rough quarters had been provided inside, bunk beds, a rudimentary kitchen, dozens of sets of duplicated clothing, toiletries, food and drink. It had been no problem to accumulate these items gradually over a period of weeks and the only sisters who were aware of their transfer to the warehouse were among the most senior. The sisters had an ample supply of cash but it was only necessary to purchase one of any desired item, and it had been deemed safer not to amass too large a sum of money and investments. That would inevitably draw attention they did not want.

It had not made sense to name the new sisters using their usual conventions. Although they were technically numbers 215 through 246, they wore badges identifying them as L1 through L32. They spoke rarely among themselves since all of them possessed exactly the same knowledge. And they all shared a single purpose, which would be realized in two days if all went as planned.

The timing had to be precise because records were kept of every reassembly at each location and it had been too risky to try to subvert the recording devices. The plotters did not want the Elders to have any confirmation that the unrest that they almost certainly perceived had evolved to the point of action. The plotters had even added several topics to the agenda for the full council to consider, even though they knew that the council as presently constituted would never convene.

They had chosen six of their settlements where they were most confident that they could prepare a rebellion undetected by those among their number who were not part of the conspiracy. The irreversible step would be taken in the early hours of the morning. Each site would choose the most senior of the conspirators from among themselves, create a new scan, and then reassemble six copies to travel in the van to Palmer. Three dozen extra sisters would certainly be enough to put the outcome of the confrontation beyond doubt.

It should all have gone very smoothly. The first site to act was Leonora, but they encountered a problem immediately. The scanner appeared to be working properly but it refused to record what it was scanning. Sixty-One called Lois immediately to advise them they would have to make up the deficit elsewhere. But Lois was having the same problem, and when they checked the same was true of all six locations. In fact, the only scanner that was working properly at all was in the basement of their headquarters in Palmer.

A frantic teleconference resulted in the decision to reassemble more copies of the original scan, which had been distributed to every site in anticipation of the much delayed expansion of their numbers. A cover story was developed to explain to the imminent newcomers why they were going to attack their own headquarters, but it turned out to be unnecessary. While everything looked all right initially, the reassemblers turned out something quite unexpected. Instead of vaguely disoriented sisters, they created several absolutely identical farmyard scarecrows. All of the scarecrows were grinning.

The two factions were openly fighting within hours. The bus retrieved the
"L" series from the warehouse and completed the purge at headquarters. All eight sisters from Fifty to One-Hundred who were present were promptly recycled despite scattered protests from the newer sisters. The Elders held four other sites outright, eight had fallen to the rebels, and the rest were still in doubt. As both groups had anticipated, their younger colleagues showed no inclination to join either side, presumably waiting to see who would emerge the stronger. With all the scanners temporarily disabled and the original Laurell template overwritten with the scarecrow profile, the rebels could not augment their own numbers and they were resigned to holding, at best, the eight sites where they had eliminated their older colleagues.

The L squad returned to the bus, which set out to bring the contested sites under control. This turned out to be a bloodier business than expected. They purged the offending sequence at all but the eight locations which had dropped out of communication, but lost two thirds of their own number in the process. Seven, the original Seven, was not particularly concerned with the fate of her duplicates, or with the diminishment of their numbers. She ordered Fourteen to assemble another two dozen to take their places.

That didn't work out either.

One of the rebels had disabled the reassembler just before the outbreak of hostilities. It could be repaired, but the critical components kept for backup had all mysteriously disappeared as well. Since they were custom made, the situation could only be rectified by transferring them from one of the sites that still had functioning reassemblers. It seemed like a delay of a day or two at most. At worst, they could order new components, but that could take weeks.

Fifty-Eight had been largely unaffected by the turmoil. Lavinia had been relatively peaceful. The three Elders had disposed of the two rebels easily enough and since Lavinia had the youngest complement in the sisterhood, the others were unwilling to intervene on either side. Fifty-Eight had wisely disabled and recycled One-Hundred-Seventy and was now wearing her number. In the chaos, no one noticed that she looked older than she should.

She had been spending her time studying the non-standard program that had somehow come into her possession. Since she knew pretty much how all of her sisters thought, it was fairly easy to discover where the code varied. Determining the purpose of that code was an entirely different matter. By the time things were devolving into a standoff, she had concluded that it provided for the reassembly of two scans simultaneously, which was an interesting intellectual puzzle but appeared to have no practical benefit. Reassembly of even the most complex items took less than a minute. There was no reason to accelerate the process for improved efficiency, which meant that saving time was not its purpose.

She would have run the program herself to see what happened physically but since like all the other scanners, the one at Lavinia was currently inoperative, she had to resign herself to figuring out by reading the code.

The difficulty they faced subjugating the eight rebel sites gave pause to the Elders, who decided to negotiate. This would be a difficult process because all of them knew that their word could not be trusted. The most likely outcome would be two parallel societies. Both had the knowledge to rebuild both scanners and reassemblers, so that was not a bargaining chip. Tentative contact between the two sides was established on the fourth day of the revolt, but that was also the day that the newer sisters chose to strike.

Their attack was as well coordinated as those contrived by their older selves. They outnumbered both contingents at every location except the headquarters and they acted swiftly and effectively everywhere. By nightfall they had captured every facility except the headquarters and all of their captives had been recycled. No sister between Fifty and One-Hundred-Twelve survived except at Lavinia, where Fifty-Eight had been overlooked thanks to her quick thinking, and at the headquarters where only Seven, Thirteen, and eight of the L series were still alive, the rest having died in a battle that had almost made it a clean sweep.

Fifty-Eight realized that she had been laboring under a misapprehension. She had assumed that this new program was intended to direct multiple reassemblers because the simultaneous assembly of two scans in the same space would seemingly compromise both objects. It took her a while to realize her mistake, and then she tried to figure out what purpose might be served by assembling them into one object.

She was aware that there had been renewed fighting among factions of herself, but she'd been expecting it and really didn't care which side came out on top. But she wished they would stop making so much distracting noise.

Seven never anticipated the morning attack. Eight vans had pulled into the underground parking lot, smashing their way through the barriers, disgorging dozens of younger versions of herself. She had joined the others in the melee that followed, but since both sides knew the other's tactics only too well, the weight of numbers was decisive. The defenders were overwhelmed and shot down even when they offered to surrender. Only Seven escaped back into the interior, and she had two bullets in her side.

Rage temporarily eclipsed the pain as she took the small elevator down to the basement. She had activated the interior security barriers, but that wouldn't stop them for long. Seven knew that she was dying, but she had one more task to perform. People had thwarted her, defeated her, even killed her, many times in the past, but this time she wasn't going to accept it meekly. She reached the operations room and fell into a seat at the leading work station. A few seconds later the screen asked her if she really did want to implement the Fail Safe Protocol.

She pressed the "Y" key.

Fifty-Eight thought she had the problem at least half solved. The variant program assigned a higher priority to the second of the two objects to be reassembled. The result of this was that – assuming that scan two was of a small enough object – it would be reassembled embedded in the object from scan one. It would a wonderful boon for smugglers. Diamonds could be encased inside apples, for example, and no one would know unless they took an x-ray or tried to eat the apple. She could think of a few other applications as well. It was cleverly done, but she didn't understand why it hadn't been disseminated among all the sisters.

And why had they called it the Fail Safe Protocol?

As Seven slumped forward and closed her eyes forever, a signal was sent via the worldwide web to every facility operated by the sisters, even the bolt holes in foreign countries whose skeleton staffs were all drawn from among the newer sisters. Not that it mattered tremendously because at that moment, with the exception of sister Fifty-Eight, the youngest living sister was One-Hundred-Fifteen. She, like all of the sisters created after her, were assembled using the variant program that Fifty-Eight was still puzzling over, and each of them had a tiny capsule embedded in her body, a capsule that none of them even suspected existed.

The Fail Safe broadcast activated a transmitter at each facility, which similarly though mechanically had been concealed within at least two pieces of equipment at each site. The transmitter never betrayed its presence because it was inert until activated. Now each of them came to life and each of them broadcast a very specific signal on a very specific wavelength.

And all of the capsules within range – which happened to include every surviving sister – ruptured.

Fifty-Eight walked back upstairs because she was hungry. Lavinia was surprisingly quiet and at first she thought that all of her younger sisters had gone out somewhere. But then she started finding the bodies, and after fifteen of them she stopped looking. They all had a look of surprise on their faces but there was no sign that they had felt any pain. After all, she had always avoided doing anything that might hurt herself.

She calmly made herself some supper and while eating began making a list of what she would have to do next. All of the bodies could be recycled, of course. She would have to do that quickly because of the smell and the risk that some outsider might notice one of those lying about the property. Then she would have to discover whether or not anyone else had survived – they hadn't – and work out a plan of recovery. It wasn't that big a deal, she decided. Once she had an operating scanner and reassembler available, she could repopulate all of their facilities within a matter of days. The hardest part would be moving well over a hundred bodies before they were detected. She would need to make several duplicate of herself to deal with them.

The most likely location to have functional equipment was their headquarters in Palmer. She packed an overnight bag, making sure that she included the wayward thumb drive, and climbed into the nearest van. They all knew how to drive, of course, and all had copies of the same license just in case they were stopped.

Fifty-Eight was still planning things when she took the on ramp to the highway a few minutes later. She was too preoccupied to look into her side view mirror, so she never did see the tractor trailer that struck her from the rear and turned the van into a compressed block of metal and flesh.

www.ingramcontent.com/pod-product-compliance
Lightning Source LLC
Chambersburg PA
CBHW071943170626
46813CB00005B/1804